The Return

The Return

Joseph Conrad

ET REMOTISSIMA PROPE

Hesperus Classics

Hesperus Classics
Published by Hesperus Press Limited
4 Rickett Street, London sw6 1ru
www.hesperuspress.com

First published in 1898 in *Tales of Unrest*
First published by Hesperus Press Limited, 2004

Foreword © Colm Tóibín, 2004

Designed and typeset by Fraser Muggeridge
Printed in Italy by Graphic Studio Srl

isbn: 1-84391-078-0

CONTENTS

Foreword by Colm Tóibín   vii

The Return   1

Biographical note   75

FOREWORD

In the last years of the nineteenth century a number of writers who were in exile in England began, as outsiders, to consider the drama surrounding the brittleness of English manners and morals and the pressures on English stability. This offered them an alluring and mysterious and, at times, evasive subject. Henry James, for example, remained fascinated by the English system of inheritance in which, on the death of her husband, the widow was cast aside while her son inherited the property. James sought to dramatise this in *The Spoils of Poynton*, published in 1896, in which all the characters are English. He was also interested, during the same period, in English forms of adultery and unfaithfulness which he dealt with in such novels as *The Other House* (1896) and *What Maisie Knew* (1897). His English characters lack the fluidity and yearning of his Americans; they are practical and rooted in the real world and only too ready to be treacherous to it should the need arise.

It was this world, too, which Oscar Wilde described in his comedies of manners written in the early 1890s, work in which no Irish characters appeared, in which members of the English drawing-room class are mimicked and mocked, masked and unmasked. So, too, the hero, whoever he is, of Robert Louis Stevenson's *The Strange Case of Dr Jekyll and Mr Hyde* (1886) wallowed in the great unstable openness of London. The vast and various city, in all its ineffable mystery and otherness, offered these three writers an escape from their own narrow heritage, and a richly layered world to chart in its duplicity, and perhaps even its decline.

This close attention to English manners did not last long. James, once the new century had begun, returned to writing about Americans in Europe. Stevenson escaped to a more exotic landscape where he died in 1894. Wilde was destroyed by the very forces which he mocked. The house of England, in all its glory, was not their property; they stayed as guests, watchful and untrusting; they used its rooms while it suited them and noticed the values of the owners and the view from the windows only as an outsider might.

Joseph Conrad, the great outsider who settled in England in 1894, the year before he published his first novel, was deeply interested in a small number of writers both in French and English whose work he studied carefully. Among these writers was Henry James. The relationship between his fiction and that of James may not seem obvious, despite the fact that, as Leon Edel has pointed out, Conrad's *Heart of Darkness* (written 1899; published 1902) bears strange similarities in structure and tone, if not in content, to James's *The Turn of the Screw* (1898).

Conrad had sent James his second book, *An Outcast of the Islands,* in 1896 with an elaborately flattering inscription. James admired the book and responded by sending him *The Spoils of Poynton*. Conrad thought that 'the delicacy and tenuity' of James's novel 'was a great sheet of plate glass – you don't know it's there till you run against it'. Ford Madox Ford reported 'the rapturous and shouting enthusiasm of Conrad over the story' and suggested that it 'must have been the high water mark of Conrad's enthusiasm for the work of any other writer'. The two men met for lunch in London in February 1897. James was fifty-three; Conrad thirty-nine. The piece of fiction which Conrad attempted immediately after their meeting was his story *The Return*, which is his most clearly Jamesian in tone and content, his most directly English in manner and background.

Conrad worked over and over on this story; the writing caused him a great deal of difficulty. When it was finished, no magazine would print it. The story, he wrote, 'embittered five months' of his life. He moved from admiring it, to disliking it, to feeling a strange protective pride towards it. In his introduction to *Tales of Unrest*, where it first appeared, he called it 'a left-handed production'. The story, he pointed out, consisted 'for the most part of physical impressions; impressions of sound and sight… rendered as if for their own sake and combined with a sublimated description of a desirable middle-class town-residence which somehow manages to produce a sinister effect'.

The story's sinister effect derives from the almost dismissive and quite reductive terms in which the contours of Alvan Hervey's comfortable and complacent life are set, versus his astonishingly rich, slow and detailed response to his wife's letter, his every move infused with poetic significance, every nuance of feeling full of shading and careful emotional manipulation. His wife's letter turns an unreflective Dr Jekyll into a Mr Hyde deeply haunted by essential and savage questions about existence; turns an orderly London household into a place of wild feeling, at times comic, and then unbearable in its despair. 'Truth would be of no use' to Hervey in the face of passion which is 'the unpardonable and secret infamy of our hearts, a thing to curse, to hide and to deny; a shameless and forlorn thing that tramples upon the smiling promises, that tears off the placid mask, that strips the body of life'. Conrad reduced his fashionable Londoner, who enjoyed 'the delightful world of crescents and squares', to becoming a man who 'stood alone, naked and afraid, like the first man on the first day of evil'.

For Conrad's men, women remain a great alluring mystery; sexual attraction moving towards guileless, puzzled obsession is a theme for him even in his later fiction. In stories such as 'A Smile of Fortune' (1911) or 'The Planter of Malata' (1914), a woman, unobtainable and strange, unsettles and then unmasks a hardened hero. In the latter story, she is 'fresh from the thick twilight of four million people and the artificiality of several London seasons'. Nonetheless, 'he felt himself in the presence of a mysterious being in whom spoke an unknown voice, like the voice of oracles, bringing everlasting unrest to the heart'.

The Return is Conrad in his most exotic territory: a house in London, not a boat in sight, utterly free of the Orient. It is set in 'the impenetrable and polished discretions of closed doors and curtained windows'. Mirrors and a carpet replace sky and sea. It is easy to imagine Conrad's friend John Galsworthy, or indeed Henry James himself, utterly at home with this material. The story itself would be enough for them, the small drama of it. But for Conrad, the slightest glance, the smallest passing moment, and words themselves, all came weighted with unfathomable implications, signals to us that time is merely the mercy of eternity. Writing for him was a way to make this both clear and mysterious, bring it home to us and move it beyond us, just as his wife's return and her pale words make Hervey conscious of matters which perhaps only an exile from English mores and manners could see: 'the revealing night... the darkness that tries the hearts, in the night useless for the work of men, but in which their gaze, undazzled by the sunshine of covetous days, wanders sometimes as far as the stars'.

– Colm Tóibín, 2004

The Return

The inner circle train from the City rushed impetuously out of a black hole and pulled up with a discordant, grinding racket in the smirched twilight of a West-End station. A line of doors flew open and a lot of men stepped out headlong. They had high hats, healthy pale faces, dark overcoats and shiny boots; they held in their gloved hands thin umbrellas and hastily folded evening papers that resembled stiff, dirty rags of greenish, pinkish, or whitish colour. Alvan Hervey stepped out with the rest, a smouldering cigar between his teeth. A disregarded little woman in rusty black, with both arms full of parcels, ran along in distress, bolted suddenly into a third-class compartment and the train went on. The slamming of carriage doors burst out sharp and spiteful like a fusillade; an icy draught mingled with acrid fumes swept the whole length of the platform and made a tottering old man, wrapped up to his ears in a woollen comforter, stop short in the moving throng to cough violently over his stick. No one spared him a glance.

Alvan Hervey passed through the ticket gate. Between the bare walls of a sordid staircase men clambered rapidly; their backs appeared alike – almost as if they had been wearing a uniform; their indifferent faces were varied but somehow suggested kinship, like the faces of a band of brothers who through prudence, dignity, disgust, or foresight would resolutely ignore each other; and their eyes, quick or slow; their eyes gazing up the dusty steps; their eyes brown, black, grey, blue, had all the same stare, concentrated and empty, satisfied and unthinking.

Outside the big doorway of the street they scattered in all directions, walking away fast from one another with the hurried air of men fleeing from something compromising; from familiarity or confidences; from something suspected and concealed – like truth or pestilence. Alvan Hervey hesitated, standing alone in the doorway for a moment, then decided to walk home.

He strode firmly. A misty rain settled like silvery dust on clothes, on moustaches; wetted the faces, varnished the flagstones, darkened the walls, dripped from umbrellas. And he moved on in the rain with careless serenity, with the tranquil ease of someone successful and disdainful, very sure of himself – a man with lots of money and friends. He was tall, well set up, good-looking and healthy; and his clear pale face had under its commonplace refinement that slight tinge of overbearing brutality which is given by the possession of only partly difficult accomplishments; by excelling in games, or in the art of making money; by the easy mastery over animals and over needy men.

He was going home much earlier than usual, straight from the City and without calling at his club. He considered himself well connected, well educated and intelligent. Who doesn't? But his connections, education and intelligence were strictly on a par with those of the men with whom he did business or amused himself. He had married five years ago. At the time all his acquaintances had said he was very much in love; and he had said so himself, frankly, because it is very well understood that every man falls in love once in his life – unless his wife dies, when it may be quite praiseworthy to fall in love again. The girl was healthy, tall, fair, and in his opinion was well connected, well educated and intelligent. She was also intensely bored with her home, where, as if packed in a tight box, her individuality – of which she was very conscious – had no play. She strode like a grenadier, was strong and upright like an obelisk, had a beautiful face, a candid brow, pure eyes, and not a thought of her own in her head. He surrendered quickly to all those charms, and she appeared to him so unquestionably of the right sort that he did not hesitate for a moment to declare himself in love. Under the cover of that sacred and poetical fiction he desired her masterfully, for various reasons; but principally for the satisfaction of having his own way. He was very dull and solemn about it – for no earthly reason, unless to conceal his feelings – which is an eminently proper thing to do. Nobody, however, would have been shocked had he neglected that duty, for the feeling he experienced really was a longing – a longing stronger and a little more complex no doubt, but no more reprehensible in its nature than a hungry man's appetite for his dinner.

After their marriage they busied themselves, with marked success, in enlarging the circle of their acquaintance. Thirty people knew them by sight; twenty more with smiling demonstrations tolerated their occasional presence within hospitable thresholds; at least fifty others became aware of their existence. They moved in their enlarged world amongst perfectly delightful men and women who feared emotion, enthusiasm, or failure, more than fire, war, or mortal disease; who tolerated only the commonest formulas of commonest thoughts, and recognised only profitable facts. It was an extremely charming sphere, the abode of all the virtues, where nothing is realised and where all joys and sorrows are cautiously toned down into pleasures and annoyances. In that serene region, then, where noble sentiments are cultivated in sufficient profusion to conceal the pitiless materialism of thoughts and aspirations, Alvan Hervey and his wife spent five years of prudent bliss unclouded by any doubt as to the moral propriety of their existence. She, to give her individuality fair play, took up all manner of philanthropic work and became a member of various rescuing and reforming societies patronised or presided over by ladies of title. He took an active interest in politics; and having met quite by chance a literary man – who nevertheless was related to an earl – he was induced to finance a moribund society paper. It was a semi-political, and wholly scandalous publication, redeemed by excessive dullness; and as it was utterly faithless, as it contained no new thought, as it never by any chance had a flash of wit, satire, or indignation in its pages, he judged it respectable enough, at first sight. Afterwards, when it paid, he promptly perceived that upon the whole it was a virtuous undertaking. It paved the way of his ambition; and he enjoyed also the special kind of importance he derived from this connection with what he imagined to be literature.

This connection still further enlarged their world. Men who wrote or drew prettily for the public came at times to their house, and his editor came very often. He thought him rather an ass because he had such big front teeth (the proper thing is to have small, even teeth) and wore his hair a trifle longer than most men do. However, some dukes wear their hair long, and the fellow indubitably knew his business. The worst was that his gravity, though perfectly portentous, could not be trusted. He sat, elegant and bulky, in the drawing room, the head of his stick hovering in front of his big teeth, and talked for hours with a thick-lipped smile (he said nothing that could be considered objectionable and not quite the thing), talked in an unusual manner – not obviously – irritatingly. His fore-head was too lofty – unusually so – and under it there was a straight nose, lost between the hairless cheeks, that in a smooth curve ran into a chin shaped like the end of a snow-shoe. And in this face that resembled the face of a fat and fiendishly knowing baby there glittered a pair of clever, peering, unbelieving black eyes. He wrote verses too. Rather an ass. But the band of men who trailed at the skirts of his monumental frock coat seemed to perceive wonderful things in what he said. Alvan Hervey put it down to affectation. Those artist chaps, upon the whole, were so affected. Still, all this was highly proper – very useful to him – and his wife seemed to like it – as if she also had derived some distinct and secret advantage from this intellectual connection. She received her mixed and decorous guests with a kind of tall, ponderous grace, peculiarly her own and which awakened in the mind of intimidated strangers incongruous and improper remin-iscences of an elephant, a giraffe, a gazelle; of a Gothic tower, of an overgrown angel. Her Thursdays were becoming famous in their world; and their world grew steadily, annexing street after street. It included also Somebody's Gardens, a crescent – a couple of squares.

Thus Alvan Hervey and his wife for five prosperous years lived by the side of one another. In time they came to know each other sufficiently well for all the practical purposes of such an existence, but they were no more capable of real intimacy than two animals feeding at the same manger, under the same roof, in a luxurious stable. His longing was appeased and became a habit; and she had her desire – the desire to get away from under the paternal roof, to assert her individuality, to move in her own set (so much smarter than the parental one); to have a home of her own, and her own share of the world's respect, envy, and applause. They understood each other warily, tacitly, like a pair of cautious conspirators in a profitable plot; because they were both unable to look at a fact, a sentiment, a principle, or a belief otherwise than in the light of their own dignity, of their own glorification, of their own advantage. They skimmed over the surface of life hand in hand, in a pure and frosty atmosphere – like two skilful skaters cutting figures on thick ice for the admiration of the beholders, and disdainfully ignoring the hidden stream, the stream restless and dark; the stream of life, profound and unfrozen.

Alvan Hervey turned twice to the left, once to the right, walked along two sides of a square, in the middle of which groups of tame-looking trees stood in respectable captivity behind iron railings, and rang at his door. A parlourmaid opened. A fad of his wife's, this, to have only women servants. That girl, while she took his hat and overcoat, said something which made him look at his watch. It was five o'clock, and his wife not at home. There was nothing unusual in that. He said, 'No; no tea,' and went upstairs.

He ascended without footfalls. Brass rods glimmered all up the red carpet. On the first-floor landing a marble woman, decently covered from neck to instep with stone draperies, advanced a row of lifeless toes to the edge of the pedestal, and thrust out blindly a rigid white arm holding a cluster of lights. He had artistic tastes – at home. Heavy curtains caught back, half concealed dark corners. On the rich, stamped paper of the walls hung sketches, water-colours, engravings. His tastes were distinctly artistic. Old church towers peeped above green masses of foliage; the hills were purple, the sands yellow, the seas sunny, the skies blue. A young lady sprawled with dreamy eyes in a moored boat, in company of a lunch basket, a champagne bottle, and an enamoured man in a blazer. Bare-legged boys flirted sweetly with ragged maidens, slept on stone steps, gambolled with dogs. A pathetically lean girl flattened against a blank wall, turned up expiring eyes and tendered a flower for sale; while, near by, the large photographs of some famous and mutilated bas-reliefs seemed to represent a massacre turned into stone.

He looked, of course, at nothing, ascended another flight of stairs and went straight into the dressing room. A bronze dragon nailed by the tail to a bracket writhed away from the wall in calm convolutions, and held, between the conventional fury of its jaws, a crude gas flame that resembled a butterfly. The room was empty, of course; but, as he stepped in, it became filled all at once with a stir of many people; because the strips of glass on the doors of wardrobes and his wife's large pier-glass reflected him from head to foot, and multiplied his image into a crowd of gentlemanly and slavish imitators who were dressed exactly like himself; had the same restrained and rare gestures; who moved when he moved, stood still with him in an obsequious immobility, and had just such appearances of life and feeling as he thought it dignified and safe for any man to manifest. And like real people who are slaves of common thoughts, that are not even their own, they affected a shadowy independence by the superficial variety of their movements. They moved together with him; but they either advanced to meet him, or walked away from him; they appeared, disappeared; they seemed to dodge behind walnut furniture, to be seen again, far within the polished panes, stepping about distinct and unreal in the convincing illusion of a room. And like the men he respected they could be trusted to do nothing individual, original, or startling – nothing unforeseen and nothing improper.

He moved for a time aimlessly in that good company, humming a popular but refined tune, and thinking vaguely of a business letter from abroad which had to be answered on the morrow with cautious prevarication. Then, as he walked towards a wardrobe, he saw appearing at his back, in the high mirror, the corner of his wife's dressing table, and amongst the glitter of silver-mounted objects on it, the square white patch of an envelope. It was such an unusual thing to be seen there that he spun round almost before he realised his surprise; and all the sham men about him pivoted on their heels; all appeared surprised; and all moved rapidly towards envelopes on dressing tables.

He recognised his wife's handwriting and saw that the envelope was addressed to himself. He muttered, 'How very odd,' and felt annoyed. Apart from any odd action being essentially an indecent thing in itself, the fact of his wife indulging in it made it doubly offensive. That she should write to him at all, when she knew he would be home for dinner, was perfectly ridiculous; but that she should leave it like this – in evidence for chance discovery – struck him as so outrageous that, thinking of it, he experienced suddenly a staggering sense of insecurity, an absurd and bizarre flash of a notion that the house had moved a little under his feet. He tore the envelope open, glanced at the letter, and sat down in a chair near by.

He held the paper before his eyes and looked at half a dozen lines scrawled on the page, while he was stunned by a noise meaningless and violent, like the clash of gongs or the beating of drums; a great aimless uproar that, in a manner, prevented him from hearing himself think and made his mind an absolute blank. This absurd and distracting tumult seemed to ooze out of the written words, to issue from between his very fingers that trembled, holding the paper. And suddenly he dropped the letter as though it had been something hot, or venomous, or filthy; and rushing to the window with the unreflecting precipitation of a man anxious to raise an alarm of fire or murder, he threw it up and put his head out.

A chill gust of wind, wandering through the damp and sooty obscurity over the waste of roofs and chimney pots, touched his face with a clammy flick. He saw an illimitable darkness, in which stood a black jumble of walls, and, between them, the many rows of gaslights stretched far away in long lines, like strung-up beads of fire. A sinister loom as of a hidden conflagration lit up faintly from below the mist, falling upon a billowy and motionless sea of tiles and bricks. At the rattle of the opened window the world seemed to leap out of the night and confront him, while floating up to his ears there came a sound vast and faint; the deep mutter of something immense and alive. It penetrated him with a feeling of dismay and he gasped silently. From the cab-stand in the square came distinct hoarse voices and a jeering laugh which sounded ominously harsh and cruel. It sounded threatening. He drew his head in, as if before an aimed blow, and flung the window down quickly. He made a few steps, stumbled against a chair, and with a great effort, pulled himself together to lay hold of a certain thought that was whizzing about loose in his head.

He got it at last, after more exertion than he expected; he was flushed, and puffed a little as though he had been catching it with his hands, but his mental hold on it was weak, so weak that he judged it necessary to repeat it aloud – to hear it spoken firmly – in order to ensure a perfect measure of possession. But he was unwilling to hear his own voice – to hear any sound whatever – owing to a vague belief, shaping itself slowly within him, that solitude and silence are the greatest felicities of mankind. The next moment it dawned upon him that they are perfectly unattainable – that faces must be seen, words spoken, thoughts heard. All the words – all the thoughts!

He said very distinctly, and looking at the carpet, 'She's gone.'

It was terrible – not the fact but the words; the words charged with the shadowy might of a meaning that seemed to possess the tremendous power to call Fate down upon the earth, like those strange and appalling words that sometimes are heard in sleep. They vibrated round him in a metallic atmosphere, in a space that had the hardness of iron and the resonance of a bell of bronze. Looking down between the toes of his boots he seemed to listen thoughtfully to the receding wave of sound; to the wave spreading out in a widening circle, embracing streets, roofs, church steeples, fields – and travelling away, widening endlessly, far, very far, where he could not hear – where he could not imagine anything – where…

'And – with that… ass,' he said again without stirring in the least. And there was nothing but humiliation. Nothing else. He could derive no moral solace from any aspect of the situation, which radiated pain only on every side. Pain. What kind of pain? It occurred to him that he ought to be heartbroken; but in an exceedingly short moment he perceived that his suffering was nothing of so trifling and dignified a kind. It was altogether a more serious matter, and partook rather of the nature of those subtle and cruel feelings which are awakened by a kick or a horse-whipping.

He felt very sick – physically sick – as though he had bitten through something nauseous. Life, that to a well-ordered mind should be a matter of congratulation, appeared to him, for a second or so, perfectly intolerable. He picked up the paper at his feet, and sat down with the wish to think it out, to understand why his wife – his wife! – should leave him, should throw away respect, comfort, peace, decency, position – throw away everything for nothing! He set himself to think out the hidden logic of her action – a mental undertaking fit for the leisure hours of a madhouse, though he couldn't see it. And he thought of his wife in every relation except the only fundamental one. He thought of her as a well-bred girl, as a wife, as a cultured person, as the mistress of a house, as a lady; but he never for a moment thought of her simply as a woman.

Then a fresh wave, a raging wave of humiliation, swept through his mind, and left nothing there but a personal sense of undeserved abasement. Why should he be mixed up with such a horrid exposure! It annihilated all the advantages of his well-ordered past, by a truth effective and unjust like a calumny – and the past was wasted. Its failure was disclosed – a distinct failure, on his part, to see, to guard, to understand. It could not be denied; it could not be explained away, hustled out of sight. He could not sit on it and look solemn. Now – if she had only died!

If she had only died! He was driven to envy such a respectable bereavement, and one so perfectly free from any taint of misfortune that even his best friend or his best enemy would not have felt the slightest thrill of exultation. No one would have cared. He sought comfort in clinging to the contemplation of the only fact of life that the resolute efforts of mankind had never failed to disguise in the clatter and glamour of phrases. And nothing lends itself more to lies than death. If she had only died! Certain words would have been said to him in a sad tone, and he, with proper fortitude, would have made appropriate answers. There were precedents for such an occasion. And no one would have cared. If she had only died! The promises, the terrors, the hopes of eternity, are the concern of the corrupt dead; but the obvious sweetness of life belongs to living, healthy men. And life was his concern: that sane and gratifying existence untroubled by too much love or by too much regret. She had interfered with it; she had defaced it. And suddenly it occurred to him he must have been mad to marry. It was too much in the nature of giving yourself away, of wearing – if for a moment – your heart on your sleeve. But everyone married. Was all mankind mad!

In the shock of that startling thought he looked up, and saw to the left, to the right, in front, men sitting far off in chairs and looking at him with wild eyes – emissaries of a distracted mankind intruding to spy upon his pain and his humiliation. It was not to be borne. He rose quickly, and the others jumped up, too, on all sides. He stood still in the middle of the room as if discouraged by their vigilance. No escape! He felt something akin to despair. Everybody must know. The servants must know tonight. He ground his teeth… And he had never noticed, never guessed anything. Everyone will know. He thought: 'The woman's a monster, but everybody will think me a fool;' and standing still in the midst of severe walnut-wood furniture, he felt such a tempest of anguish within him that he seemed to see himself rolling on the carpet, beating his head against the wall. He was disgusted with himself, with the loathsome rush of emotion breaking through all the reserves that guarded his manhood. Something unknown, withering and poisonous, had entered his life, passed near him, touched him, and he was deteriorating. He was appalled. What was it? She was gone. Why? His head was ready to burst with the endeavour to understand her act and his subtle horror of it. Everything was changed. Why? Only a woman gone, after all; and yet he had a vision, a vision quick and distinct as a dream: the vision of everything he had thought indestructible and safe in the world crashing down about him, like solid walls do before the fierce breath of a hurricane. He stared, shaking in every limb, while he felt the destructive breath, the mysterious breath, the breath of passion, stir the profound peace of the house. He looked round in fear. Yes. Crime may be forgiven; uncalculating sacrifice, blind trust, burning faith, other follies, may be turned to account; suffering, death itself, may with a grin or a frown be explained away; but passion is the unpardonable and secret infamy of our hearts, a thing to curse, to hide and to deny; a shameless and forlorn thing that tramples upon the smiling promises, that tears off the placid mask, that strips the body of life. And it had come to him! It had laid its unclean hand upon the spotless draperies of his existence, and he had to face it alone with all the world looking on. All the world! And he thought that even the bare suspicion of such an adversary within his house carried with it a taint and a condemnation. He put both his hands out as if to ward off the reproach of a defiling truth; and, instantly, the appalled conclave of unreal men, standing about mutely beyond the clear lustre of mirrors, made at him the same gesture of rejection and horror.

He glanced vainly here and there, like a man looking in desperation for a weapon or for a hiding place, and understood at last that he was disarmed and cornered by the enemy that, without any squeamishness, would strike so as to lay open his heart. He could get help nowhere, or even take counsel with himself, because in the sudden shock of her desertion the sentiments which he knew that in fidelity to his bringing up, to his prejudices and his surroundings, he ought to experience, were so mixed up with the novelty of real feelings, of fundamental feelings that know nothing of creed, class, or education, that he was unable to distinguish clearly between what is and what ought to be; between the inexcusable truth and the valid pretences. And he knew instinctively that truth would be of no use to him. Some kind of concealment seemed a necessity because one cannot explain. Of course not! Who would listen? One had simply to be without stain and without reproach to keep one's place in the forefront of life.

He said to himself, 'I must get over it the best I can,' and began to walk up and down the room. What next? What ought to be done? He thought: 'I will travel – no I won't. I shall face it out.' And after that resolve he was greatly cheered by the reflection that it would be a mute and an easy part to play, for no one would be likely to converse with him about the abominable conduct of – that woman. He argued to himself that decent people – and he knew no others – did not care to talk about such indelicate affairs. She had gone off – with that unhealthy, fat ass of a journalist. Why? He had been all a husband ought to be. He had given her a good position – she shared his prospects – he had treated her invariably with great consideration. He reviewed his conduct with a kind of dismal pride. It had been irreproachable. Then, why? For love? Profanation! There could be no love there. A shameful impulse of passion. Yes, passion. His own wife! Good God!… And the indelicate aspect of his domestic misfortune struck him with such shame that, next moment, he caught himself in the act of pondering absurdly over the notion whether it would not be more dignified for him to induce a general belief that he had been in the habit of beating his wife. Some fellows do… and anything would be better than the filthy fact, for it was clear he had lived with the root of it for five years – and it was too shameful. Anything! Anything! Brutality… But he gave it up directly, and began to think of the divorce court. It did not present itself to him, notwithstanding his respect for law and usage, as a proper refuge for dignified grief. It appeared rather as an unclean and sinister cavern where men and women are haled by adverse fate to writhe ridiculously in the presence of uncompromising truth. It should not be allowed. That woman! Five… years… married five years… and never to see anything. Not to the very last day… not till she coolly went off. And he pictured to himself all the people he knew engaged in speculating as to whether all that time he had been blind, foolish, or infatuated. What a woman! Blind!… Not at all. Could a clean-minded man imagine such depravity? Evidently not. He drew a free breath. That was the attitude to take; it was dignified enough; it gave him the advantage, and he could not help perceiving that it was moral. He yearned unaffectedly to see morality (in his person) triumphant before the world. As to her, she would be forgotten. Let her be forgotten – buried in oblivion – lost! No one would allude… Refined people – and every man and woman he knew could be so described – had, of course, a horror of such topics. Had they? Oh, yes. No one would allude to her… in his hearing. He stamped his foot, tore the letter across, then again and again. The thought of sympathising friends excited in him a fury of mistrust. He flung down the small bits of paper. They settled, fluttering at his feet, and looked very white on the dark carpet, like a scattered handful of snowflakes.

This fit of hot anger was succeeded by a sudden sadness, by the darkening passage of a thought that ran over the scorched surface of his heart, like upon a barren plain, and after a fiercer assault of sunrays, the melancholy and cooling shadow of a cloud. He realised that he had had a shock – not a violent or rending blow that can be seen, resisted, returned, forgotten, but a thrust, insidious and penetrating, that had stirred all those feelings, concealed and cruel, which the arts of the devil, the fears of mankind – God's infinite compassion, perhaps – keep chained deep down in the inscrutable twilight of our breasts. A dark curtain seemed to rise before him, and for less than a second he looked upon the mysterious universe of moral suffering. As a landscape is seen complete, and vast, and vivid, under a flash of lightning, so he could see disclosed in a moment all the immensity of pain that can be contained in one short moment of human thought. Then the curtain fell again, but his rapid vision left in Alvan Hervey's mind a trail of invincible sadness, a sense of loss and bitter solitude, as though he had been robbed and exiled. For a moment he ceased to be a member of society with a position, a career, and a name attached to all this, like a descriptive label of some complicated compound. He was a simple human being removed from the delightful world of crescents and squares. He stood alone, naked and afraid, like the first man on the first day of evil. There are in life events, contacts, glimpses, that seem brutally to bring all the past to a close. There is a shock and a crash, as of a gate flung to behind one by the perfidious hand of Fate. Go and seek another paradise, fool or sage. There is a moment of dumb dismay, and the wanderings must begin again; the painful explaining away of facts, the feverish raking up of illusions, the cultivation of a fresh crop of lies in the sweat of one's brow, to sustain life, to make it supportable, to make it fair, so as to hand intact to another generation of blind wanderers the charming legend of a heartless country, of a promised land, all flowers and blessings...

He came to himself with a slight start, and became aware of an oppressive, crushing desolation. It was only a feeling, it is true, but it produced on him a physical effect, as though his chest had been squeezed in a vice. He perceived himself so extremely forlorn and lamentable, and was moved so deeply by the oppressive sorrow, that another turn of the screw, he felt, would bring tears out of his eyes. He was deteriorating. Five years of life in common had appeased his longing. Yes, long time ago. The first five months did that – but... There was the habit – the habit of her person, of her smile, of her gestures, of her voice, of her silence. She had a pure brow and good hair. How utterly wretched all this was. Good hair and fine eyes – remarkably fine. He was surprised by the number of details that intruded upon his unwilling memory. He could not help remembering her footsteps, the rustle of her dress, her way of holding her head, her decisive manner of saying 'Alvan', the quiver of her nostrils when she was annoyed. All that had been so much his property, so intimately and specially his! He raged in a mournful, silent way, as he took stock of his losses. He was like a man counting the cost of an unlucky speculation – irritated, depressed – exasperated with himself and with others, with the fortunate, with the indifferent, with the callous; yet the wrong done him appeared so cruel that he would perhaps have dropped a tear over that spoliation if it had not been for his conviction that men do not weep. Foreigners do; they also kill sometimes in such circumstances. And to his horror he felt himself driven to regret almost that the usages of a society ready to forgive the shooting of a burglar forbade him, under the circumstances, even as much as a thought of murder. Nevertheless, he clenched his fists and set his teeth hard. And he was afraid at the same time. He was afraid with that penetrating faltering fear that seems, in the very middle of a beat, to turn one's heart into a handful of dust. The contamination of her crime spread out, tainted the universe, tainted himself; woke up all the dormant infamies of the world; caused a ghastly kind of clairvoyance in which he could see the towns and fields of the earth, its sacred places, its temples and its houses, peopled by monsters – by monsters of duplicity, lust, and murder. She was a monster – he himself was thinking monstrous thoughts… and yet he was like other people. How many men and women at this very moment were plunged in abominations – meditated crimes. It was frightful to think of. He remembered all the streets – the well-to-do streets he had passed on his way home; all the innumerable houses with closed doors and curtained windows. Each seemed now an abode of anguish and folly. And his thought, as if appalled, stood still, recalling with dismay the decorous and frightful silence that was like a conspiracy; the grim, impenetrable silence of miles of walls concealing passions, misery, thoughts of crime. Surely he was not the only man; his was not the only house… and yet no one knew – no one guessed. But he knew. He knew with unerring certitude that could not be deceived by the correct silence of walls, of closed doors, of curtained windows. He was beside himself with a despairing agitation, like a man informed of a deadly secret – the secret of a calamity threatening the safety of mankind – the sacredness, the peace of life.

He caught sight of himself in one of the looking glasses. It was a relief. The anguish of his feeling had been so powerful that he more than half expected to see some distorted wild face there, and he was pleasantly surprised to see nothing of the kind. His aspect, at any rate, would let no one into the secret of his pain. He examined himself with attention. His trousers were turned up, and his boots a little muddy, but he looked very much as usual. Only his hair was slightly ruffled, and that disorder, somehow, was so suggestive of trouble that he went quickly to the table, and began to use the brushes, in an anxious desire to obliterate the compromising trace, that only vestige of his emotion. He brushed with care, watching the effect of his smoothing; and another face, slightly pale and more tense than was perhaps desirable, peered back at him from the toilet glass. He laid the brushes down, and was not satisfied. He took them up again and brushed, brushed mechanically – forgot himself in that occupation. The tumult of his thoughts ended in a sluggish flow of reflection, such as, after the outburst of a volcano, the almost imperceptible progress of a stream of lava, creeping languidly over a convulsed land and pitilessly obliterating any landmark left by the shock of the earthquake. It is a destructive but, by comparison, it is a peaceful phenomenon. Alvan Hervey was almost soothed by the deliberate pace of his thoughts. His moral landmarks were going one by one, consumed in the fire of his experience, buried in hot mud, in ashes. He was cooling – on the surface; but there was enough heat left somewhere to make him slap the brushes on the table, and turning away, say in a fierce whisper: 'I wish him joy… Damn the woman!'

He felt himself utterly corrupted by her wickedness, and the most significant symptom of his moral downfall was the bitter, acrid satisfaction with which he recognised it. He, deliberately, swore in his thoughts; he meditated sneers; he shaped in profound silence words of cynical unbelief, and his most cherished convictions stood revealed finally as the narrow prejudices of fools. A crowd of shapeless, unclean thoughts crossed his mind in a stealthy rush, like a band of veiled malefactors hastening to a crime. He put his hands deep into his pockets. He heard a faint ringing somewhere, and muttered to himself: 'I am not the only one… not the only one.' There was another ring. Front door!

His heart leapt up into his throat, and forthwith descended as low as his boots. A call! Who? Why? He wanted to rush out on the landing and shout to the servant: 'Not at home! Gone away abroad!'…Any excuse. He could not face a visitor. Not this evening. No. Tomorrow… Before he could break out of the numbness that enveloped him like a sheet of lead, he heard far below, as if in the entrails of the earth, a door close heavily. The house vibrated to it more than to a clap of thunder. He stood still, wishing himself invisible. The room was very chilly. He did not think he would ever feel like that. But people must be met – they must be faced – talked to – smiled at. He heard another door, much nearer – the door of the drawing room – being opened and flung to again. He imagined for a moment he would faint. How absurd! That kind of thing had to be gone through. A voice spoke. He could not catch the words. Then the voice spoke again, and footsteps were heard on the first-floor landing. Hang it all! Was he to hear that voice and those footsteps whenever anyone spoke or moved? He thought: 'This is like being haunted – I suppose it will last for a week or so, at least. Till I forget. Forget! Forget!' Someone was coming up the second flight of stairs. Servant? He listened, then, suddenly, as though an incredible, frightful revelation had been shouted to him from a distance, he bellowed out in the empty room: 'What! What!' in such a fiendish tone as to astonish himself. The footsteps stopped outside the door. He stood open-mouthed, maddened and still, as if in the midst of a catastrophe. The door handle rattled lightly. It seemed to him that the walls were coming apart, that the furniture swayed at him; the ceiling slanted queerly for a moment, a tall wardrobe tried to topple over. He caught hold of something and it was the back of a chair. So he had reeled against a chair! Oh! Confound it! He gripped hard.

The flaming butterfly poised between the jaws of the bronze dragon radiated a glare, a glare that seemed to leap up all at once into a crude, blinding fierceness, and made it difficult for him to distinguish plainly the figure of his wife standing upright with her back to the closed door. He looked at her and could not detect her breathing. The harsh and violent light was beating on her, and he was amazed to see her preserve so well the composure of her upright attitude in that scorching brilliance which, to his eyes, enveloped her like a hot and consuming mist. He would not have been surprised if she had vanished in it as suddenly as she had appeared. He stared and listened; listened for some sound, but the silence round him was absolute – as though he had in a moment grown completely deaf as well as dim-eyed. Then his hearing returned, preternaturally sharp. He heard the patter of a rain shower on the window panes behind the lowered blinds, and below, far below, in the artificial abyss of the square, the deadened roll of wheels and the splashy trotting of a horse. He heard a groan also – very distinct – in the room – close to his ear.

He thought with alarm: 'I must have made that noise myself;' and at the same instant the woman left the door, stepped firmly across the floor before him, and sat down in a chair. He knew that step. There was no doubt about it. She had come back! And he very nearly said aloud, 'Of course!' – such was his sudden and masterful perception of the indestructible character of her being. Nothing could destroy her – and nothing but his own destruction could keep her away. She was the incarnation of all the short moments which every man spares out of his life for dreams, for precious dreams that concrete the most cherished, the most profitable of his illusions. He peered at her with inward trepidation. She was mysterious, significant, full of obscure meaning – like a symbol. He peered, bending forward, as though he had been discovering about her things he had never seen before. Unconsciously he made a step towards her – then another. He saw her arm make an ample, decided movement and he stopped. She had lifted her veil. It was like the lifting of a visor.

The spell was broken. He experienced a shock as though he had been called out of a trance by the sudden noise of an explosion. It was even more startling and more distinct; it was an infinitely more intimate change, for he had the sensation of having come into this room only that very moment; of having returned from very far; he was made aware that some essential part of himself had in a flash returned into his body, returned finally from a fierce and lamentable region, from the dwelling place of unveiled hearts. He woke up to an amazing infinity of contempt, to a droll bitterness of wonder, to a disenchanted conviction of safety. He had a glimpse of the irresistible force, and he saw also the barrenness of his convictions – of her convictions. It seemed to him that he could never make a mistake as long as he lived. It was morally impossible to go wrong. He was not elated by that certitude; he was dimly uneasy about its price; there was a chill as of death in this triumph of sound principles, in this victory snatched under the very shadow of disaster.

The last trace of his previous state of mind vanished, as the instantaneous and elusive trail of a bursting meteor vanishes on the profound blackness of the sky; it was the faint flicker of a painful thought, gone as soon as perceived, that nothing but her presence – after all – had the power to recall him to himself. He stared at her. She sat with her hands on her lap, looking down; and he noticed that her boots were dirty, her skirts wet and splashed, as though she had been driven back there by a blind fear through a waste of mud. He was indignant, amazed and shocked, but in a natural, healthy way now; so that he could control those unprofitable sentiments by the dictates of cautious self-restraint. The light in the room had no unusual brilliance now; it was a good light in which he could easily observe the expression of her face. It was that of dull fatigue. And the silence that surrounded them was the normal silence of any quiet house, hardly disturbed by the faint noises of a respectable quarter of the town. He was very cool – and it was quite coolly that he thought how much better it would be if neither of them ever spoke again. She sat with closed lips, with an air of lassitude in the stony forgetfulness of her pose, but after a moment she lifted her drooping eyelids and met his tense and inquisitive stare by a look that had all the formless eloquence of a cry. It penetrated, it stirred without informing; it was the very essence of anguish stripped of words that can be smiled at, argued away, shouted down, disdained. It was anguish naked and unashamed, the bare pain of existence let loose upon the world in the fleeting unreserve of a look that had in it an immensity of fatigue, the scornful sincerity, the black impudence of an extorted confession. Alvan Hervey was seized with wonder, as though he had seen something inconceivable; and some obscure part of his being was ready to exclaim with him: 'I would never have believed it!' but an instantaneous revulsion of wounded susceptibilities checked the unfinished thought.

He felt full of rancorous indignation against the woman who could look like this at one. This look probed him; it tampered with him. It was dangerous to one as would be a hint of unbelief whispered by a priest in the august decorum of a temple; and at the same time it was impure, it was disturbing, like a cynical consolation muttered in the dark, tainting the sorrow, corroding the thought, poisoning the heart. He wanted to ask her furiously: 'Who do you take me for? How dare you look at me like this?' He felt himself helpless before the hidden meaning of that look; he resented it with pained and futile violence as an injury so secret that it could never, never be redressed. His wish was to crush her by a single sentence. He was stainless. Opinion was on his side; morality, men and gods were on his side; law, conscience – all the world! She had nothing but that look. And he could only say:

'How long do you intend to stay here?'

Her eyes did not waver, her lips remained closed; and for any effect of his words he might have spoken to a dead woman, only that this one breathed quickly. He was profoundly disappointed by what he had said. It was a great deception, something in the nature of treason. He had deceived himself. It should have been altogether different – other words – another sensation. And before his eyes, so fixed that at times they saw nothing, she sat apparently as unconscious as though she had been alone, sending that look of brazen confession straight at him – with an air of staring into empty space. He said significantly:

'Must I go then?' And he knew he meant nothing of what he implied.

One of her hands on her lap moved slightly as though his words had fallen there and she had thrown them off on the floor. But her silence encouraged him. Possibly it meant remorse – perhaps fear. Was she thunderstruck by his attitude?... Her eyelids dropped. He seemed to understand ever so much – everything! Very well – but she must be made to suffer. It was due to him. He understood everything, yet he judged it indispensable to say with an obvious affectation of civility:

'I don't understand – be so good as to...'

She stood up. For a second he believed she intended to go away, and it was as though someone had jerked a string attached to his heart. It hurt. He remained open-mouthed and silent. But she made an irresolute step towards him, and instinctively he moved aside. They stood before one another, and the fragments of the torn letter lay between them – at their feet – like an insurmountable obstacle, like a sign of eternal separation! Around them three other couples stood still and face to face, as if waiting for a signal to begin some action – a struggle, a dispute, or a dance.

She said: 'Don't – Alvan!' and there was something that resembled a warning in the pain of her tone. He narrowed his eyes as if trying to pierce her with his gaze. Her voice touched him. He had aspirations after magnanimity, generosity, superiority – interrupted, however, by flashes of indignation and anxiety – frightful anxiety to know how far she had gone. She looked down at the torn paper. Then she looked up, and their eyes met again, remained fastened together, like an unbreakable bond, like a clasp of eternal complicity; and the decorous silence, the pervading quietude of the house which enveloped this meeting of their glances became for a moment inexpressibly vile, for he was afraid she would say too much and make magnanimity impossible, while behind the profound mournfulness of her face there was a regret –

a regret of things done – the regret of delay – the thought that if she had only turned back a week sooner – a day sooner – only an hour sooner… They were afraid to hear again the sound of their voices; they did not know what they might say – perhaps something that could not be recalled; and words are more terrible than facts. But the tricky fatality that lurks in obscure impulses spoke through Alvan Hervey's lips suddenly; and he heard his own voice with the excited and sceptical curiosity with which one listens to actors' voices speaking on the stage in the strain of a poignant situation.

'If you have forgotten anything… of course… I…'

Her eyes blazed at him for an instant; her lips trembled – and then she also became the mouthpiece of the mysterious force forever hovering near us; of that perverse inspiration, wandering capricious and uncontrollable, like a gust of wind.

'What is the good of this, Alvan?… You know why I came back… You know that I could not…'

He interrupted her with irritation.

'Then – what's this?' he asked, pointing downwards at the torn letter.

'That's a mistake,' she said hurriedly, in a muffled voice.

This answer amazed him. He remained speechless, staring at her. He had half a mind to burst into a laugh. It ended in a smile as involuntary as a grimace of pain.

'A mistake…' he began, slowly, and then found himself unable to say another word.

'Yes… it was honest,' she said very low, as if speaking to the memory of a feeling in a remote past.

He exploded.

'Curse your honesty!… Is there any honesty in all this!… When did you begin to be honest? Why are you here? What are you now?… Still honest?…'

He walked at her, raging, as if blind; during these three quick strides he lost touch of the material world and was whirled interminably through a kind of empty universe made up of nothing but fury and anguish, till he came suddenly upon her face – very close to his. He stopped short, and all at once seemed to remember something heard ages ago.

'You don't know the meaning of the word,' he shouted.

She did not flinch. He perceived with fear that everything around him was still. She did not move a hair's breadth; his own body did not stir. An imperturbable calm enveloped their two motionless figures, the house, the town, all the world – and the trifling tempest of his feelings. The violence of the short tumult within him had been such as could well have shattered all creation; and yet nothing was changed. He faced his wife in the familiar room in his own house. It had not fallen. And right and left all the innumerable dwellings, standing shoulder to shoulder, had resisted the shock of his passion, had presented, unmoved, to the loneliness of his trouble, the grim silence of walls, the impenetrable and polished discretion of closed doors and curtained windows. Immobility and silence pressed on him, assailed him, like two accomplices of the immovable and mute woman before his eyes. He was suddenly vanquished. He was shown his impotence. He was soothed by the breath of a corrupt resignation coming to him through the subtle irony of the surrounding peace.

He said with villainous composure:

'At any rate it isn't enough for me. I want to know more – if you're going to stay.'

'There is nothing more to tell,' she answered, sadly.

It struck him as so very true that he did not say anything. She went on:

'You wouldn't understand… .'

'No?' he said, quietly. He held himself tight, not to burst into howls and imprecations.

'I tried to be faithful…' she began again.

'And this?' he exclaimed, pointing at the fragments of her letter.

'This – this is a failure,' she said.

'I should think so,' he muttered, bitterly.

'I tried to be faithful to myself – Alvan – and… and honest to you…'

'If you had tried to be faithful to me it would have been more to the purpose,' he interrupted, angrily. 'I've been faithful to you and you have spoiled my life – both our lives…' Then after a pause the unconquerable preoccupation of self came out, and he raised his voice to ask resentfully, 'And, pray, for how long have you been making a fool of me?'

She seemed horribly shocked by that question. He did not wait for an answer, but went on moving about all the time; now and then coming up to her, then wandering off restlessly to the other end of the room.

'I want to know. Everybody knows, I suppose, but myself – and that's your honesty!'

'I have told you there is nothing to know,' she said, speaking unsteadily as if in pain. 'Nothing of what you suppose. You don't understand me. This letter is the beginning – and the end.'

'The end – this thing has no end,' he clamoured, unexpectedly. 'Can't you understand that? I can… The beginning…' He stopped and looked into her eyes with concentrated intensity, with a desire to see, to penetrate, to understand, that made him positively hold his breath till he gasped.

'By heavens!' he said, standing perfectly still in a peering attitude and within less than a foot from her. 'By heavens!' he repeated, slowly, and in a tone whose involuntary strangeness was a complete mystery to himself. 'By heavens – I could believe you – I could believe anything – now!'

He turned short on his heel and began to walk up and down the room with an air of having disburdened himself of the final pronouncement of his life – of having said something on which he would not go back, even if he could. She remained as if rooted to the carpet. Her eyes followed the restless movements of the man, who avoided looking at her. Her wide stare clung to him, enquiring, wondering and doubtful.

'But the fellow was forever sticking in here,' he burst out, distractedly. 'He made love to you, I suppose – and, and…' He lowered his voice. 'And – you let him.'

'And I let him,' she murmured, catching his intonation, so that her voice sounded unconscious, sounded far off and slavish, like an echo.

He said twice, 'You! You!' violently, then calmed down. 'What could you see in the fellow?' he asked, with unaffected wonder. 'An effeminate, fat ass. What could you... Weren't you happy? Didn't you have all you wanted? Now – frankly; did I deceive your expectations in any way? Were you disappointed with our position – or with our prospects – perhaps? You know you couldn't be – they are much better than you could hope for when you married me...'

He forgot himself so far as to gesticulate a little while he went on with animation:

'What could you expect from such a fellow? He's an outsider – a rank outsider... If it hadn't been for my money... do you hear?... for my money, he wouldn't know where to turn. His people won't have anything to do with him. The fellow's no class – no class at all. He's useful, certainly, that's why I... I thought you had enough intelligence to see it... And you... No! It's incredible! What did he tell you? Do you care for no one's opinion – is there no restraining influence in the world for you – women? Did you ever give me a thought? I tried to be a good husband. Did I fail? Tell me – what have I done?'

Carried away by his feelings he took his head in both his hands and repeated wildly:

'What have I done?... Tell me! What?...'

'Nothing,' she said.

'Ah! You see... you can't...' he began, triumphantly, walking away; then suddenly, as though he had been flung back at her by something invisible he had met, he spun round and shouted with exasperation:

'What on earth did you expect me to do?'

Without a word she moved slowly towards the table, and, sitting down, leant on her elbow, shading her eyes with her hand. All that time he glared at her watchfully as if expecting every moment to find in her deliberate movements an answer to his question. But he could not read anything, he could gather no hint of her thought. He tried to suppress his desire to shout, and after waiting a while, said with incisive scorn:

'Did you want me to write absurd verses; to sit and look at you for hours – to talk to you about your soul? You ought to have known I wasn't that sort… I had something better to do. But if you think I was totally blind…'

He perceived in a flash that he could remember an infinity of enlightening occurrences. He could recall ever so many distinct occasions when he came upon them; he remembered the absurdly interrupted gesture of his fat, white hand, the rapt expression of her face, the glitter of unbelieving eyes; snatches of incomprehensible conversations not worth listening to, silences that had meant nothing at the time and seemed now illuminating like a burst of sunshine. He remembered all that. He had not been blind. Oh! No! And to know this was an exquisite relief: it brought back all his composure.

'I thought it beneath me to suspect you,' he said, loftily.

The sound of that sentence evidently possessed some magical power, because, as soon as he had spoken, he felt wonderfully at ease; and directly afterwards he experienced a flash of joyful amazement at the discovery that he could be inspired to such noble and truthful utterance. He watched the effect of his words. They caused her to glance to him quickly over her shoulder. He caught a glimpse of wet eyelashes, of a red cheek with a tear running down swiftly; and then she turned away again and sat as before, covering her face with her hands.

'You ought to be perfectly frank with me,' he said, slowly.

'You know everything,' she answered, indistinctly, through her fingers.

'This letter… Yes… but…'

'And I came back,' she exclaimed in a stifled voice; 'you know everything.'

'I am glad of it – for your sake,' he said, with impressive gravity. He listened to himself with solemn emotion. It seemed to him that something inexpressibly momentous was in progress within the room, that every word and every gesture had the importance of events preordained from the beginning of all things, and summing up in their finality the whole purpose of creation.

'For your sake,' he repeated.

Her shoulders shook as though she had been sobbing, and he forgot himself in the contemplation of her hair. Suddenly he gave a start, as if waking up, and asked very gently and not much above a whisper:

'Have you been meeting him often?'

'Never!' she cried into the palms of her hands.

This answer seemed for a moment to take from him the power of speech. His lips moved for some time before any sound came.

'You preferred to make love here – under my very nose,' he said, furiously. He calmed down instantly, and felt regretfully uneasy, as though he had let himself down in her estimation by that outburst. She rose, and with her hand on the back of the chair confronted him with eyes that were perfectly dry now. There was a red spot on each of her cheeks.

'When I made up my mind to go to him – I wrote,' she said.

'But you didn't go to him,' he took up in the same tone. 'How far did you go? What made you come back?'

'I didn't know myself,' she murmured. Nothing of her moved but her lips. He fixed her sternly.

'Did he expect this? Was he waiting for you?' he asked.

She answered him by an almost imperceptible nod, and he continued to look at her for a good while without making a sound. Then, at last –

'And I suppose he is waiting yet?' he asked, quickly.

Again she seemed to nod at him. For some reason he felt he must know the time. He consulted his watch gloomily. Half-past seven.

'Is he?' he muttered, putting the watch in his pocket. He looked up at her, and, as if suddenly overcome by a sense of sinister fun, gave a short, harsh laugh, directly repressed.

'No! It's the most unheard!…' he mumbled, while she stood before him biting her lower lip, as if plunged in deep thought. He laughed again in one low burst that was as spiteful as an imprecation. He did not know why he felt such an overpowering and sudden distaste for the facts of existence – for facts in general – such an immense disgust at the thought of all the many days already lived through. He was wearied. Thinking seemed a labour beyond his strength. He said:

'You deceived me – now you make a fool of him… It's awful! Why?'

'I deceived myself!' she exclaimed.

'Oh! Nonsense!' he said, impatiently.

'I am ready to go if you wish it,' she went on, quickly. 'It was due to you – to be told – to know. No! I could not!' she cried, and stood still wringing her hands stealthily.

'I am glad you repented before it was too late,' he said, in a dull tone and looking at his boots. 'I am glad… some spark of better feeling,' he muttered, as if to himself. He lifted up his head after a moment of brooding silence. 'I am glad to see that there is some sense of decency left in you,' he added a little louder. Looking at her he appeared to hesitate, as if estimating the possible consequences of what he wished to say, and at last blurted out:

'After all, I loved you…'

'I did not know,' she whispered.

'Good God!' he cried. 'Why do you imagine I married you?'

The indelicacy of his obtuseness angered her.

'Ah – why?' she said through her teeth.

He appeared overcome with horror, and watched her lips intently as though in fear.

'I imagined many things,' she said, slowly, and paused. He watched, holding his breath. At last she went on musingly, as if thinking aloud, 'I tried to understand. I tried honestly… Why?… To do the usual thing – I suppose… To please yourself.'

He walked away smartly, and when he came back, close to her, he had a flushed face.

'You seemed pretty well pleased, too – at the time,' he hissed, with scathing fury. 'I needn't ask whether you loved me.'

'I know now I was perfectly incapable of such a thing,'

she said, calmly, 'If I had, perhaps you would not have married me.'

'It's very clear I would not have done it if I had known you – as I know you now.'

He seemed to see himself proposing to her – ages ago. They were strolling up the slope of a lawn. Groups of people were scattered in sunshine. The shadows of leafy boughs lay still on the short grass. The coloured sun-shades far off, passing between trees, resembled deliberate and brilliant butterflies moving without a flutter. Men smiling amiably, or else very grave, within the impeccable shelter of their black coats, stood by the side of women who, clustered in clear summer toilettes, recalled all the fabulous tales of enchanted gardens where animated flowers smile at bewitched knights. There was a sump-tuous serenity in it all, a thin, vibrating excitement, the perfect security, as of an invincible ignorance, that evoked within him a transcendent belief in felicity as the lot of all mankind, a recklessly picturesque desire to get promptly something for himself only, out of that splendour unmarred by any shadow of a thought. The girl walked by his side across an open space; no one was near, and suddenly he stood still, as if inspired, and spoke. He remembered looking at her pure eyes, at her candid brow; he remembered glancing about quickly to see if they were being observed, and thinking that nothing could go wrong in a world of so much charm, purity, and distinction. He was proud of it. He was one of its makers, of its possessors, of its guardians, of its extollers. He wanted to grasp it solidly, to get as much gratification as he could out of it; and in view of its incomparable quality, of its unstained atmosphere, of its nearness to the heaven of its choice, this gust of brutal desire seemed the most noble of aspirations. In a second he lived again through all these moments, and then all the pathos of his failure presented itself to him with such vividness that there was a suspicion of tears in his tone when he said almost unthinkingly, 'My God! I did love you!'

She seemed touched by the emotion of his voice. Her lips quivered a little, and she made one faltering step towards him, putting out her hands in a beseeching gesture, when she perceived, just in time, that being absorbed by the tragedy of his life he had absolutely forgotten her very existence. She stopped, and her outstretched arms fell slowly. He, with his features distorted by the bitterness of his thought, saw neither her movement nor her gesture. He stamped his foot in vexation, rubbed his head – then exploded.

'What the devil am I to do now?'

He was still again. She seemed to understand, and moved to the door firmly.

'It's very simple – I'm going,' she said aloud.

At the sound of her voice he gave a start of surprise, looked at her wildly, and asked in a piercing tone:

'You… Where? To him?'

'No – alone – goodbye.'

The door handle rattled under her groping hand as though she had been trying to get out of some dark place.

'No – stay!' he cried.

She heard him faintly. He saw her shoulder touch the lintel of the door. She swayed as if dazed. There was less than a second of suspense while they both felt as if poised on the very edge of moral annihilation, ready to fall into some devouring nowhere. Then, almost simultaneously, he shouted, 'Come back!' and she let go the handle of the door. She turned round in peaceful desperation like one who deliberately has thrown away the last chance of life; and, for a moment, the room she faced appeared terrible, and dark, and safe – like a grave.

He said, very hoarse and abrupt: 'It can't end like this… Sit down,' and while she crossed the room again to the low-backed chair before the dressing table, he opened the door and put his head out to look and listen. The house was quiet. He came back pacified, and asked:

'Do you speak the truth?'

She nodded.

'You have lived a lie, though,' he said, suspiciously.

'Ah! You made it so easy,' she answered.

'You reproach me – me!'

'How could I?' she said; 'I would have you no other – now.'

'What do you mean by…' he began, then checked himself, and without waiting for an answer went on, 'I won't ask any questions. Is this letter the worst of it?'

She had a nervous movement of her hands.

'I must have a plain answer,' he said, hotly.

'Then, no! The worst is my coming back.'

There followed a period of dead silence, during which they exchanged searching glances.

He said authoritatively:

'You don't know what you are saying. Your mind is unhinged. You are beside yourself, or you would not say such things. You can't control yourself. Even in your remorse…' He paused a moment, then said with a doctoral air: 'Self-restraint is everything in life, you know. It's happiness, it's dignity… it's everything.'

She was pulling nervously at her handkerchief while he went on watching anxiously to see the effect of his words. Nothing satisfactory happened. Only, as he began to speak again, she covered her face with both her hands.

'You see where the want of self-restraint leads to. Pain – humiliation – loss of respect – of friends, of everything that ennobles life, that… All kinds of horrors,' he concluded, abruptly.

She made no stir. He looked at her pensively for some time as though he had been concentrating the melancholy thoughts evoked by the sight of that abased woman. His eyes became fixed and dull. He was profoundly penetrated by the solemnity of the moment; he felt deeply the greatness of the occasion. And more than ever the walls of his house seemed to enclose the sacredness of ideals to which he was about to offer a magnificent sacrifice. He was the high priest of that temple, the severe guardian of formulas, of rites, of the pure ceremonial concealing the black doubts of life. And he was not alone. Other men, too – the best of them – kept watch and ward by the hearthstones that were the altars of that profitable persuasion. He understood confusedly that he was part of an immense and beneficent power, which had a reward ready for every discretion. He dwelt within the invincible wisdom of silence; he was protected by an indestructible faith that would last forever, that would withstand unshaken all the assaults – the loud execrations of apostates, and the secret weariness of its confessors! He was in league with a universe of untold advantages. He represented the moral strength of a beautiful reticence that could vanquish all the deplorable crudities of life – fear, disaster, sin – even death itself. It seemed to him he was on the point of sweeping triumphantly away all the illusory mysteries of existence. It was simplicity itself.

'I hope you see now the folly – the utter folly of wickedness,' he began in a dull, solemn manner. 'You must respect the conditions of your life or lose all it can give you. All! Everything!'

He waved his arm once, and three exact replicas of his face, of his clothes, of his dull severity, of his solemn grief, repeated the wide gesture that in its comprehensive sweep indicated an infinity of moral sweetness, embraced the walls, the hangings, the whole house, all the crowd of houses outside, all the flimsy and inscrutable graves of the living, with their doors numbered like the doors of prison cells, and as impenetrable as the granite of tombstones.

'Yes! Restraint, duty, fidelity – unswerving fidelity to what is expected of you. This – only this – secures the reward, the peace. Everything else we should labour to subdue – to destroy. It's misfortune; it's disease. It is terrible – terrible. We must not know anything about it – we needn't. It is our duty to ourselves – to others. You do not live all alone in the world – and if you have no respect for the dignity of life, others have. Life is a serious matter. If you don't conform to the highest standards you are no one – it's a kind of death. Didn't this occur to you? You've only to look round you to see the truth of what I am saying. Did you live without noticing anything, without understanding anything? From a child you had examples before your eyes – you could see daily the beauty, the blessings of morality, of principles…'

His voice rose and fell pompously in a strange chant. His eyes were still, his stare exalted and sullen; his face was set, was hard, was woodenly exulting over the grim inspiration that secretly possessed him, seethed within him, lifted him up into a stealthy frenzy of belief. Now and then he would stretch out his right arm over her head, as it were, and he spoke down at that sinner from a height, and with a sense of avenging virtue, with a profound and pure joy as though he could from his steep pinnacle see every weighty word strike and hurt like a punishing stone.

'Rigid principles – adherence to what is right,' he finished after a pause.

'What is right?' she said, distinctly, without uncovering her face.

'Your mind is diseased!' he cried, upright and austere. 'Such a question is rot – utter rot. Look round you – there's your answer, if you only care to see. Nothing that outrages the received beliefs can be right. Your conscience tells you that. They are the received beliefs because they are the best, the noblest, the only possible. They survive…'

He could not help noticing with pleasure the philosophic breadth of his view, but he could not pause to enjoy it, for his inspiration, the call of august truth, carried him on.

'You must respect the moral foundations of a society that has made you what you are. Be true to it. That's duty – that's honour – that's honesty.'

He felt a great glow within him, as though he had

44

swallowed something hot. He made a step nearer. She sat up and looked at him with an ardour of expectation that stimulated his sense of the supreme importance of that moment. And as if forgetting himself he raised his voice very much.

' "What's right?" you ask me. Think only. What would you have been if you had gone off with that infernal vagabond?… What would you have been?… You! My wife!…'

He caught sight of himself in the pier glass, drawn up to his full height, and with a face so white that his eyes, at the distance, resembled the black cavities in a skull. He saw himself as if about to launch imprecations, with arms uplifted above her bowed head. He was ashamed of that unseemly posture, and put his hands in his pockets hurriedly. She murmured faintly, as if to herself:

'Ah! What am I now?'

'As it happens you are still Mrs Alvan Hervey – uncommonly lucky for you, let me tell you,' he said in a conversational tone. He walked up to the furthest corner of the room, and, turning back, saw her sitting very upright, her hands clasped on her lap, and with a lost, unswerving gaze of her eyes which stared unwinking like the eyes of the blind, at the crude gas flame, blazing and still, between the jaws of the bronze dragon.

He came up quite close to her, and straddling his legs a little, stood looking down at her face for some time without taking his hands out of his pockets. He seemed to be turning over in his mind a heap of words, piecing his next speech out of an overpowering abundance of thoughts.

'You've tried me to the utmost,' he said at last; and as soon as he said these words he lost his moral footing, and felt himself swept away from his pinnacle by a flood of passionate resentment against the bungling creature that had come so near to spoiling his life. 'Yes; I've been tried more than any man ought to be,' he went on with righteous bitterness. 'It was unfair. What possessed you to?… What possessed you?… Write such a… After five years of perfect happiness! 'Pon my word, no one would believe… Didn't you feel you couldn't? Because you couldn't… it was impossible – you know. Wasn't it? Think. Wasn't it?'

'It was impossible,' she whispered, obediently.

This submissive assent given with such readiness did not soothe him, did not elate him; it gave him, inexplicably, that sense of terror we experience when in the midst of conditions we had learnt to think absolutely safe we discover all at once the presence of a near and unsuspected danger. It was impossible, of course! He knew it. She knew it. She confessed it. It was impossible! That man knew it, too – as well as anyone; couldn't help knowing it. And yet those two had been engaged in a conspiracy against his peace – in a criminal enterprise for which there could be no sanction of belief within themselves. There could not be! There could not be! And yet how near to… With a short thrill he saw himself an exiled forlorn figure in a realm of ungovernable, of unrestrained folly. Nothing could be foreseen, foretold – guarded against. And the sensation was intolerable, had something of the withering horror that may be conceived as following upon the utter extinction of all hope. In the flash of thought the dishonouring episode seemed to disengage itself from everything actual, from earthly conditions, and even from earthly suffering; it became purely a terrifying knowledge, an annihilating knowledge of a blind and infernal force. Something desperate and vague, a flicker of an insane desire to abase himself before the mysterious impulses of evil, to ask for mercy in some way, passed through his mind; and then came the idea, the persuasion, the certitude, that the evil must be forgotten – must be resolutely ignored to make life possible; that the knowledge must be kept out of mind, out of sight, like the knowledge of certain death is kept out of the daily existence of men. He stiffened himself inwardly for the effort, and next moment it appeared very easy, amazingly feasible, if one only kept strictly to facts, gave one's mind to their perplexities and not to their meaning. Becoming conscious of a long silence, he cleared his throat warningly, and said in a steady voice:

'I am glad you feel this... uncommonly glad... you felt this in time. For, don't you see...' Unexpectedly he hesitated.

'Yes... I see,' she murmured.

'Of course you would,' he said, looking at the carpet and speaking like one who thinks of something else. He lifted his head. 'I cannot believe – even after this – even after this – that you are altogether – altogether... other than what I thought you. It seems impossible – to me.'

'And to me,' she breathed out.

'Now – yes,' he said, 'but this morning? And tomorrow?... This is what...'

He started at the drift of his words and broke off

abruptly. Every train of thought seemed to lead into the hopeless realm of ungovernable folly, to recall the knowledge and the terror of forces that must be ignored. He said rapidly:

'My position is very painful – difficult… I feel…'

He looked at her fixedly with a pained air, as though frightfully oppressed by a sudden inability to express his pent-up ideas.

'I am ready to go,' she said very low. 'I have forfeited everything… to learn… to learn…'

Her chin fell on her breast; her voice died out in a sigh. He made a slight gesture of impatient assent.

'Yes! Yes! It's all very well… of course. Forfeited – ah! Morally forfeited – only morally forfeited… if I am to believe you…'

She startled him by jumping up.

'Oh! I believe, I believe,' he said, hastily, and she sat down as suddenly as she had got up. He went on gloomily:

'I've suffered – I suffer now. You can't understand how much. So much that when you propose a parting I almost think… But no. There is duty. You've forgotten it; I never did. Before heaven, I never did. But in a horrid exposure like this the judgement of mankind goes astray – at least for a time. You see, you and I – at least I feel that – you and I are one before the world. It is as it should be. The world is right – in the main – or else it couldn't be – couldn't be – what it is. And we are part of it. We have our duty to – to our fellow beings who don't want to… to… er…'

He stammered. She looked up at him with wide eyes, and her lips were slightly parted. He went on mumbling:

'…Pain… Indignation… Sure to misunderstand. I've suffered enough. And if there has been nothing irreparable – as you assure me… then…'

'Alvan!' she cried.

'What?' he said, morosely. He gazed down at her for a moment with a sombre stare, as one looks at ruins, at the devastation of some natural disaster.

'Then,' he continued, after a short pause, 'the best thing is… the best for us… for everyone… Yes… least pain – most unselfish…' His voice faltered, and she heard only detached words. '…Duty… Burden… Ourselves… Silence.'

A moment of perfect stillness ensued.

'This is an appeal I am making to your conscience,' he said, suddenly, in an explanatory tone, 'not to add to the wretchedness of all this: to try loyally and help me to live it down somehow. Without any reservations – you know. Loyally! You can't deny I've been cruelly wronged and – after all – my affection deserves…' He paused with evident anxiety to hear her speak.

'I make no reservations,' she said, mournfully. 'How could I? I found myself out and came back to…' – her eyes flashed scornfully for an instant – '…to what – to what you propose. You see… I… I can be trusted… now.'

He listened to every word with profound attention, and when she ceased seemed to wait for more.

'Is that all you've got to say?' he asked.

She was startled by his tone, and said faintly:

'I spoke the truth. What more can I say?'

'Confound it! You might say something human,' he burst out. 'It isn't being truthful; it's being brazen – if you want to know. Not a word to show you feel your position, and – and mine. Not a single word of acknowledgement, or regret – or remorse… or… something.'

'Words!' she whispered in a tone that irritated him. He stamped his foot.

'This is awful!' he exclaimed. 'Words? Yes, words. Words mean something – yes – they do – for all this infernal affectation. They mean something to me – to everybody – to you. What the devil did you use to express those sentiments – sentiments – pah! – which made you forget me, duty, shame!'

He foamed at the mouth while she stared at him, appalled by this sudden fury. 'Did you two talk only with your eyes?' he spluttered savagely. She rose.

'I can't bear this,' she said, trembling from head to foot. 'I am going.'

They stood facing one another for a moment.

'Not you,' he said, with conscious roughness, and began to walk up and down the room. She remained very still with an air of listening anxiously to her own heartbeats, then sank down on the chair slowly, and sighed, as if giving up a task beyond her strength.

'You misunderstand everything I say,' he began quietly, 'but I prefer to think that – just now – you are not account-able for your actions.' He stopped again before her. 'Your mind is unhinged,' he said, with unction. 'To go now would be adding crime – yes, crime – to folly. I'll have no scandal in my life, no matter what the cost. And why? You are sure to misunderstand me – but I'll tell you. As a matter of duty. Yes. But you're sure to misunderstand me – recklessly. Women always do – they are too – too narrow-minded.'

He waited for a while, but she made no sound, didn't even look at him; he felt uneasy, painfully uneasy, like a man who suspects he is unreasonably mistrusted. To combat that exasperating sensation he recommenced talking very fast. The sound of his words excited his thoughts, and in the play of darting thoughts he had glimpses now and then of the inexpugnable rock of his convictions, towering in solitary grandeur above the unprofitable waste of errors and passions.

'For it is self-evident,' he went on, with anxious vivacity, 'it is self-evident that, on the highest ground we haven't the right – no, we haven't the right to intrude our miseries upon those who – who naturally expect better things from us. Everyone wishes his own life and the life around him to be beautiful and pure. Now, a scandal amongst people of our position is disastrous for the morality – a fatal influence – don't you see – upon the general tone of the class – very important – the most important, I verily believe, in – in the community. I feel this – profoundly. This is the broad view. In time you'll give me… when you become again the woman I loved – and trusted…'

He stopped short, as though unexpectedly suffocated, then in a completely changed voice said, 'For I did love and trust you' – and again was silent for a moment. She put her handkerchief to her eyes.

'You'll give me credit for – for – my motives. It's mainly loyalty to – to the larger conditions of our life – where you – you! of all women – failed. One doesn't usually talk like this – of course – but in this case you'll admit… And consider – the innocent suffer with the guilty. The world is pitiless in its judgements. Unfortunately there are always those in it who are only too eager to misunderstand. Before you and before my conscience I am guiltless, but any – any disclosure would impair my usefulness in the sphere – in the larger sphere in which I hope soon to… I believe you fully shared my views in that matter – I don't want to say any more… on – on that point – but, believe me, true unselfishness is to bear one's burdens in – in silence. The ideal must – must be preserved – for others, at least. It's clear as daylight. If I've a – a loathsome sore, to gratuitously display it would be abominable – abominable! And often in life – in the highest conception of life – outspokenness in certain circumstances is nothing less than criminal. Temptation, you know, excuses no one. There is no such thing really if one looks steadily to one's welfare – which is grounded in duty. But there are the weak,' – his tone became ferocious for an instant – 'and there are the fools and the envious – especially for people in our position. I am guiltless of this terrible – terrible… estrangement; but if there has been nothing irreparable,' – something gloomy, like a deep shadow passed over his face – 'nothing irreparable – you see even now I am ready to trust you implicitly – then our duty is clear.'

He looked down. A change came over his expression and straight away, from the outward impetus of his loquacity, he passed into the dull contemplation of all the appeasing truths that, not without some wonder, he had so recently been able to discover within himself. During this profound and soothing communion with his innermost beliefs he remained staring at the carpet, with a portentously solemn face and with a dull vacuity of eyes that seemed to gaze into the blankness of an empty hole. Then, without stirring in the least, he continued:

'Yes. Perfectly clear. I've been tried to the utmost, and I can't pretend that, for a time, the old feelings – the old feelings are not…' He sighed… 'But I forgive you…'

She made a slight movement without uncovering her eyes. In his profound scrutiny of the carpet he noticed nothing. And there was silence, silence within and silence without, as though his words had stilled the beat and tremor of all the surrounding life, and the house had stood alone – the only dwelling upon a deserted earth.

He lifted his head and repeated solemnly:

'I forgive you… from a sense of duty – and in the hope…'

He heard a laugh, and it not only interrupted his words but also destroyed the peace of his self-absorption with the vile pain of a reality intruding upon the beauty of a dream. He couldn't understand whence the sound came. He could see, foreshortened, the tear-stained, dolorous face of the woman stretched out, and with her head thrown over the back of the seat. He thought the piercing noise was a delusion. But another shrill peal followed by a deep sob and succeeded by another shriek of mirth positively seemed to tear him out from where he stood. He bounded to the door. It was closed. He turned the key and thought: that's no good…

'Stop this!' he cried, and perceived with alarm that he could hardly hear his own voice in the midst of her screaming. He darted back with the idea of stifling that unbearable noise with his hands, but stood still distracted, finding himself as unable to touch her as though she had been on fire. He shouted, 'Enough of this!' like men shout in the tumult of a riot, with a red face and starting eyes; then, as if swept away before another burst of laughter, he disappeared in a flash out of three looking glasses, vanished suddenly from before her. For a time the woman gasped and laughed at no one in the luminous stillness of the empty room.

He reappeared, striding at her, and with a tumbler of water in his hand. He stammered: 'Hysterics – Stop – They will hear – Drink this.' She laughed at the ceiling. 'Stop this!' he cried. 'Ah!'

He flung the water in her face, putting into the action all the secret brutality of his spite, yet still felt that it would have been perfectly excusable – in anyone – to send the tumbler after the water. He restrained himself, but at the same time was so convinced nothing could stop the horror of those mad shrieks that, when the first sensation of relief came, it did not even occur to him to doubt the impression of having become suddenly deaf. When, next moment, he became sure that she was sitting up, and really very quiet, it was as though everything – men, things, sensations – had come to a rest. He was prepared to be grateful. He could not take his eyes off her, fearing, yet unwilling to admit the possibility of her beginning again; for, the experience, however contemptuously he tried to think of it, had left the bewilderment of a mysterious terror. Her face was streaming with water and tears; there was a wisp of hair on her forehead, another stuck to her cheek; her hat was on one side, undecorously tilted; her soaked veil resembled a sordid rag festooning her forehead. There was an utter unreserve in her aspect, an abandonment of safeguards, that ugliness of truth which can only be kept out of daily life by unremitting care for appearances. He did not know why, looking at her, he thought suddenly of tomorrow, and why the thought called out a deep feeling of unutterable, discouraged weariness – a fear of facing the succession of days. Tomorrow! It was as far as yesterday. Ages elapsed between sunrises – sometimes. He scanned her features like one looks at a forgotten country. They were not distorted – he recognised landmarks, so to speak; but it was only a resemblance that he could see, not the woman of yesterday – or was it, perhaps, more than the woman of yesterday? Who could tell? Was it something new? A new expression – or a new shade of expression? or something deep – an old truth unveiled, a fundamental and hidden truth – some unnecessary, accursed certitude? He became aware that he was trembling very much, that he had an empty tumbler in his hand – that time was passing. Still looking at her with lingering mistrust he reached towards the table to put the glass down and was startled to feel it apparently go through the wood. He had missed the edge. The surprise, the slight jingling noise of the accident annoyed him beyond expression. He turned to her irritated.

'What's the meaning of this?' he asked, grimly.

She passed her hand over her face and made an attempt to get up.

'You're not going to be absurd again,' he said. ' 'Pon my soul, I did not know you could forget yourself to that extent.' He didn't try to conceal his physical disgust, because he believed it to be a purely moral reprobation of every unreserve, of anything in the nature of a scene.

'I assure you – it was revolting,' he went on. He stared for a moment at her. 'Positively degrading,' he added, with insistence.

She stood up quickly as if moved by a spring and tottered. He started forward instinctively. She caught hold of the back of the chair and steadied herself. This arrested him, and they faced each other wide-eyed, uncertain, and yet coming back slowly to the reality of things with relief and wonder, as though just awakened after tossing through a long night of fevered dreams.

'Pray, don't begin again,' he said, hurriedly, seeing her open her lips. 'I deserve some little consideration – and such unaccountable behaviour is painful to me. I expect better things... I have the right...'

She pressed both her hands to her temples.

'Oh, nonsense!' he said, sharply. 'You are perfectly capable of coming down to dinner. No one should even suspect; not even the servants. No one! No one!... I am sure you can.'

She dropped her arms; her face twitched. She looked straight into his eyes and seemed incapable of pronouncing a word. He frowned at her.

'I – wish – it,' he said, tyrannically. 'For your own sake also...' He meant to carry that point without any pity. Why didn't she speak? He feared passive resistance. She must... Make her come.

His frown deepened, and he began to think of some effectual violence, when most unexpectedly she said in a firm voice, 'Yes, I can,' and clutched the chair-back again. He was relieved, and all at once her attitude ceased to interest him. The important thing was that their life would begin again with an everyday act – with something that could not be misunderstood, that, thank God, had no moral meaning, no perplexity – and yet was symbolic of their uninterrupted communion in the past – in all the future. That morning, at that table, they had breakfast together; and now they would dine. It was all over! What had happened between could be forgotten – must be forgotten, like things that can only happen once – death for instance.

'I will wait for you,' he said, going to the door. He had some difficulty with it, for he did not remember he had turned the key. He hated that delay, and his checked impatience to be gone out of the room made him feel quite ill as, with the consciousness of her presence behind his back, he fumbled at the lock. He managed it at last; then in the doorway he glanced over his shoulder to say, 'It's rather late – you know –' and saw her standing where he had left her, with a face white as alabaster and perfectly still, like a woman in a trance.

He was afraid she would keep him waiting, but without any breathing time, he hardly knew how, he found himself sitting at table with her. He had made up his mind to eat, to talk, to be natural. It seemed to him necessary that deception should begin at home. The servants must not know – must not suspect. This intense desire of secrecy; of secrecy dark, destroying, profound, discreet like a grave, possessed him with the strength of a hallucination – seemed to spread itself to inanimate objects that had been the daily companions of his life, affected with a taint of enmity every single thing within the faithful walls that would stand forever between the shamelessness of facts and the indignation of mankind. Even when – as it happened once or twice – both the servants left the room together, he remained carefully natural, industriously hungry, laboriously at his ease, as though he had wanted to cheat the black oak sideboard, the heavy curtains, the stiff-backed chairs into the belief of an unstained happiness. He was mistrustful of his wife's self-control, unwilling to look at her and reluctant to speak, for it seemed to him inconceivable that she should not betray herself by the slightest movement, by the very first word spoken. Then he thought the silence in the room was becoming dangerous, and so excessive as to produce the effect of an intolerable uproar. He wanted to end it, as one is anxious to interrupt an indiscreet confession; but with the memory of that laugh upstairs he dared not give her an occasion to open her lips. Presently he heard her voice pronouncing in a calm tone some unimportant remark. He detached his eyes from the centre of his plate and felt excited as if on the point of looking at a wonder. And nothing could be more wonderful than her composure. He was looking at the candid eyes, at the pure brow, at what he had seen every evening for years in that place; he listened to the voice that for five years he had heard everyday. Perhaps she was a little pale – but a healthy pallor had always been for him one of her chief attractions. Perhaps her face was rigidly set – but that marmoreal impassiveness, that magnificent stolidity, as of a wonderful statue by some great sculptor working under the curse of the gods; that imposing, unthinking stillness of her features, had till then mirrored for him the tranquil dignity of a soul of which he had thought himself – as a matter of course – the inexpugnable possessor. Those were the outward signs of her difference from the ignoble herd that feels, suffers, fails, errs – but has no distinct value in the world except as a moral contrast to the prosperity of the elect. He had been proud of her appearance. It had the perfectly proper frankness of perfection – and now he was shocked to see it unchanged. She looked like this, spoke like this, exactly like this, a year ago, a month ago – only yesterday when she… What went on within made no difference. What did she think? What meant the pallor, the placid face, the candid brow, the pure eyes? What did she think during all these years? What did she think yesterday – today; what would she think tomorrow? He must find out… And yet how could he get to know? She had been false to him, to that man, to herself; she was ready to be false – for him. Always false. She looked lies, breathed lies, lived lies – would tell lies – always – to the end of life! And he would never know what she meant. Never! Never! No one could. Impossible to know.

He dropped his knife and fork, brusquely, as though by the virtue of a sudden illumination he had been made aware of poison in his plate, and became positive in his mind that he could never swallow another morsel of food as long as he lived. The dinner went on in a room that had been steadily growing, from some cause, hotter than a furnace. He had to drink. He drank time after time, and, at last, recollecting himself, was frightened at the quantity, till he perceived that what he had been drinking was water – out of two different wineglasses; and the discovered unconsciousness of his actions affected him painfully.

He was disturbed to find himself in such an unhealthy state of mind. Excess of feeling – excess of feeling; and it was part of his creed that any excess of feeling was unhealthy – morally unprofitable; a taint on practical manhood. Her fault. Entirely her fault. Her sinful self-forgetfulness was contagious. It made him think thoughts he had never had before; thoughts disintegrating, tormenting, sapping to the very core of life – like mortal disease; thoughts that bred the fear of air, of sunshine, of men – like the whispered news of a pestilence.

The maids served without noise; and to avoid looking at his wife and looking within himself, he followed with his eyes first one and then the other without being able to distinguish between them. They moved silently about, without one being able to see by what means, for their skirts touched the carpet all round; they glided here and there, receded, approached, rigid in black and white, with precise gestures, and no life in their faces, like a pair of marionettes in mourning; and their air of wooden unconcern struck him as unnatural, suspicious, irremediably hostile. That such people's feelings or judgement could affect one in any way, had never occurred to him before. He understood they had no prospects, no principles – no refinement and no power. But now he had become so debased that he could not even attempt to disguise from himself his yearning to know the secret thoughts of his servants. Several times he looked up covertly at the faces of those girls. Impossible to know. They changed his plates and utterly ignored his existence. What impenetrable duplicity. Women – nothing but women round him. Impossible to know. He experienced that heart-probing, fiery sense of dangerous loneliness which sometimes assails the courage of a solitary adventurer in an unexplored country. The sight of a man's face – he felt – of any man's face, would have been a profound relief. One would know then – something – could understand... He would engage a butler as soon as possible. And then the end of that dinner – which had seemed to have been going on for hours – the end came, taking him violently by surprise, as though he had expected in the natural course of events to sit at that table for ever and ever.

But upstairs in the drawing room, he became the victim of a restless fate, that would, on no account, permit him to sit down. She had sunk on a low easy chair, and taking up from a small table at her elbow a fan with ivory leaves, shaded her face from the fire. The coals glowed without a flame; and upon the red glow the vertical bars of the grate stood out at her feet, black and curved, like the charred ribs of a consumed sacrifice. Far off, a lamp perched on a slim brass rod, burned under a wide shade of crimson silk: the centre, within the shadows of the large room, of a fiery twilight that had in the warm quality of its tint something delicate, refined and infernal. His soft footfalls and the subdued beat of the clock on the high mantelpiece answered each other regularly – as if Time and himself, engaged in a measured contest, had been pacing together through the infernal delicacy of twilight towards a mysterious goal.

He walked from one end of the room to the other without a pause, like a traveller who, at night, hastens doggedly upon an interminable journey. Now and then he glanced at her. Impossible to know. The gross precision of that thought expressed to his practical mind something illimitable and infinitely profound, the all-embracing subtlety of a feeling, the eternal origin of his pain. This woman had accepted him, had abandoned him – had returned to him. And of all this he would never know the truth. Never. Not till death – not after – not on Judgement Day when all shall be disclosed, thoughts and deeds, rewards and punishments, but the secret of hearts alone shall return, forever unknown, to the Inscrutable Creator of good and evil, to the Master of doubts and impulses.

He stood still to look at her. Thrown back and with her face turned away from him, she did not stir – as if asleep. What did she think? What did she feel? And in the presence of her perfect stillness, in the breathless silence, he felt himself insignificant and powerless before her, like a prisoner in chains. The fury of his impotence called out sinister images, that faculty of tormenting vision, which in a moment of anguishing sense of wrong induces a man to mutter threats or make a menacing gesture in the solitude of an empty room. But the gust of passion passed at once, left him trembling a little, with the wondering, reflective fear of a man who has paused on the very verge of suicide. The serenity of truth and the peace of death can be only secured through a largeness of contempt embracing all the profitable servitudes of life. He found he did not want to know. Better not. It was all over. It was as if it hadn't been. And it was very necessary for both of them, it was morally right, that nobody should know.

He spoke suddenly, as if concluding a discussion.

'The best thing for us is to forget all this.'

She started a little and shut the fan with a click.

'Yes, forgive – and forget,' he repeated, as if to himself.

'I'll never forget,' she said in a vibrating voice. 'And I'll never forgive myself…'

'But I, who have nothing to reproach myself…' He began, making a step towards her. She jumped up.

'I did not come back for your forgiveness,' she exclaimed, passionately, as if clamouring against an unjust aspersion.

He only said, 'Oh!' and became silent. He could not understand this unprovoked aggressiveness of her attitude, and certainly was very far from thinking that an unpremeditated hint of something resembling emotion in the tone of his last words had caused that uncontrollable burst of sincerity. It completed his bewilderment, but he was not at all angry now. He was as if benumbed by the fascination of the incomprehensible. She stood before him, tall and indistinct, like a black phantom in the red twilight. At last poignantly uncertain as to what would happen if he opened his lips, he muttered:

'But if my love is strong enough…' and hesitated.

He heard something snap loudly in the fiery stillness. She had broken her fan. Two thin pieces of ivory fell, one after another, without a sound, on the thick carpet, and instinctively he stooped to pick them up. While he groped at her feet it occurred to him that the woman there had in her hands an indispensable gift which nothing else on earth could give; and when he stood up he was penetrated by an irresistible belief in an enigma, by the conviction that within his reach and passing away from him was the very secret of existence – its certitude, immaterial and precious! She moved to the door, and he followed at her elbow, casting about for a magic word that would make the enigma clear, that would compel the surrender of the gift. And there is no such word! The enigma is only made clear by sacrifice, and the gift of heaven is in the hands of every man. But they had lived in a world that abhors enigmas, and cares for no gifts but such as can be obtained in the street. She was nearing the door. He said hurriedly:

' 'Pon my word, I loved you – I love you now.'

She stopped for an almost imperceptible moment to give him an indignant glance, and then moved on. That feminine penetration – so clever and so tainted by the eternal instinct of self-defence, so ready to see an obvious evil in everything it cannot understand – filled her with bitter resentment against both the men who could offer to the spiritual and tragic strife of her feelings nothing but the coarseness of their abominable materialism. In her anger against her own ineffectual self-deception she found hate enough for them both. What did they want? What more did this one want? And as her husband faced her again, with his hand on the door handle, she asked herself whether he was unpardonably stupid, or simply ignoble.

She said nervously, and very fast:

'You are deceiving yourself. You never loved me. You wanted a wife – some woman – any woman that would think, speak, and behave in a certain way – in a way you approved. You loved yourself.'

'You won't believe me?' he asked, slowly.

'If I had believed you loved me,' she began, passionately, then drew in a long breath; and during that pause he heard the steady beat of blood in his ears, 'If I had believed it… I would never have come back,' she finished, recklessly.

He stood looking down as though he had not heard. She waited. After a moment he opened the door, and, on the landing, the sightless woman of marble appeared, draped to the chin, thrusting blindly at them a cluster of lights.

He seemed to have forgotten himself in a meditation so deep that on the point of going out she stopped to look at him in surprise. While she had been speaking he had wandered on the track of the enigma, out of the world of senses into the region of feeling. What did it matter what she had done, what she had said, if through the pain of her acts and words he had obtained the word of the enigma! There can be no life without faith and love – faith in a human heart, love of a human being! That touch of grace, whose help once in life is the privilege of the most undeserving, flung open for him the portals of beyond, and in contemplating there the certitude immaterial and precious he forgot all the meaningless accidents of existence: the bliss of getting, the delight of enjoying; all the protean and enticing forms of the cupidity that rules a material world of foolish joys, of contemptible sorrows. Faith! – Love! – the undoubting, clear faith in the truth of a soul – the great tenderness, deep as the ocean, serene and eternal, like the infinite peace of space above the short tempests of the earth. It was what he had wanted all his life – but he understood it only then for the first time. It was through the pain of losing her that the knowledge had come. She had the gift! She had the gift! And in all the world she was the only human being that could surrender it to his immense desire. He made a step forward, putting his arms out, as if to take her to his breast, and, lifting his head, was met by such a look of blank consternation that his arms fell as though they had been struck down by a blow. She started away from him, stumbled over the threshold, and once on the landing turned, swift and crouching. The train of her gown swished as it flew round her feet. It was an undisguised panic. She panted, showing her teeth, and the hate of strength, the disdain of weakness, the eternal preoccupation of sex came out like a toy demon out of a box.

'This is odious,' she screamed.

He did not stir; but her look, her agitated movements, the sound of her voice were like a mist of facts thickening between him and the vision of love and faith. It vanished; and looking at that face triumphant and scornful, at that white face, stealthy and unexpected, as if discovered staring from an ambush, he was coming back slowly to the world of senses. His first clear thought was: I am married to that woman; and the next: she will give nothing but what I see. He felt the need not to see. But the memory of the vision, the memory that abides forever within the seer made him say to her with the naive austerity of a convert awed by the touch of a new creed, 'You haven't the gift.' He turned his back on her, leaving her completely mystified. And she went upstairs slowly, struggling with a distasteful suspicion of having been confronted by something more subtle than herself – more profound than the misunderstood and tragic contest of her feelings.

He shut the door of the drawing room, and moved at hazard, alone amongst the heavy shadows and in the fiery twilight as of an elegant place of perdition. She hadn't the gift – no one had… He stepped on a book that had fallen off one of the crowded little tables. He picked up the slender volume, and holding it, approached the crimson-shaded lamp. The fiery tint deepened on the cover, and contorted gold letters sprawling all over it in an intricate maze, came out, gleaming redly. 'Thorns and Arabesques.' He read it twice, 'Thorns and Ar…' The other's book of verses. He dropped it at his feet, but did not feel the slightest pang of jealousy or indignation. What did he know?… What?… The mass of hot coals tumbled down in the grate, and he turned to look at them… Ah! That one was ready to give up everything he had for that woman – who did not come – who had not the faith, the love, the courage to come. What did that man expect, what did he hope, what did he want? The woman – or the certitude immaterial and precious! The first unselfish thought he had ever given to any human being was for that man who had tried to do him a terrible wrong. He was not angry. He was saddened by an impersonal sorrow, by a vast melancholy as of all mankind longing for what cannot be attained. He felt his fellowship with every man – even with that man – especially with that man. What did he think now? Had he ceased to wait – and hope? Would he ever cease to wait and hope? Would he understand that the woman, who had no courage, had not the gift – had not the gift!

The clock began to strike, and the deep-toned vibration filled the room as though with the sound of an enormous bell tolling far away. He counted the strokes. Twelve. Another day had begun. Tomorrow had come; the mysterious and lying tomorrow that lures men, disdainful of love and faith, on and on through the poignant futilities of life to the fitting reward of a grave. He counted the strokes, and gazing at the grate seemed to wait for more. Then, as if called out, left the room, walking firmly.

When outside he heard footsteps in the hall and stood still. A bolt was shot – then another. They were locking up – shutting out his desire and his deception from the indignant criticism of a world full of noble gifts for those who proclaim themselves without stain and without reproach. He was safe; and on all sides of his dwelling servile fears and servile hopes slept, dreaming of success, behind the severe discretion of doors as impenetrable to the truth within as the granite of tombstones. A lock snapped – a short chain rattled. Nobody shall know!

Why was this assurance of safety heavier than a burden of fear, and why the day that began presented itself obstinately like the last day of all – like a today without a tomorrow? Yet nothing was changed, for nobody would know; and all would go on as before – the getting, the enjoying, the blessing of hunger that is appeased every day; the noble incentives of unappeasable ambitions. All – all the blessings of life. All – but the certitude immaterial and precious – the certitude of love and faith. He believed the shadow of it had been with him as long as he could remember; that invisible presence had ruled his life. And now the shadow had appeared and faded he could not extinguish his longing for the truth of its substance. His desire of it was naive; it was masterful like the material aspirations that are the groundwork of existence, but, unlike these, it was unconquerable. It was the subtle despotism of an idea that suffers no rivals, that is lonely, inconsolable, and dangerous. He went slowly up the stairs. Nobody shall know. The days would go on and he would go far – very far. If the idea could not be mastered, Fortune could be, man could be – the whole world. He was dazzled by the greatness of the prospect; the brutality of a practical instinct shouted to him that only that which could be had was worth having. He lingered on the steps. The lights were out in the hall, and a small yellow flame flitted about down there. He felt a sudden contempt for himself which braced him up. He went on, but at the door of their room and with his arm advanced to open it, he faltered. On the flight of stairs below, the head of the girl who had been locking up appeared. His arm fell. He thought, 'I'll wait till she is gone' – and stepped back within the perpendicular folds of a portière.

He saw her come up gradually, as if ascending from a well. At every step the feeble flame of the candle swayed before her tired, young face, and the darkness of the hall seemed to cling to her black skirt, followed her, rising like a silent flood, as though the great night of the world had broken through the discreet reserve of walls, of closed doors, of curtained windows. It rose over the steps, it leapt up the walls like an angry wave, it flowed over the blue skies, over the yellow sands, over the sunshine of landscapes, and over the pretty pathos of ragged innocence and of meek starvation. It swallowed up the delicious idyll in a boat and the mutilated immortality of famous bas-reliefs. It flowed from outside – it rose higher, in a destructive silence. And, above it, the woman of marble, composed and blind on the high pedestal, seemed to ward off the devouring night with a cluster of lights.

He watched the rising tide of impenetrable gloom with impatience, as if anxious for the coming of a darkness black enough to conceal a shameful surrender. It came nearer. The cluster of lights went out. The girl ascended facing him. Behind her the shadow of a colossal woman danced lightly on the wall. He held his breath while she passed by, noiseless and with heavy eyelids. And on her track the flowing tide of a tenebrous sea filled the house, seemed to swirl about his feet, and rising unchecked, closed silently above his head.

The time had come but he did not open the door. All was still; and instead of surrendering to the reasonable exigencies of life he stepped out, with a rebelling heart, into the darkness of the house. It was the abode of an impenetrable night; as though indeed the last day had come and gone, leaving him alone in a darkness that has no tomorrow. And looming vaguely below, the woman of marble, livid and still like a patient phantom, held out in the night a cluster of extinguished lights.

His obedient thought traced for him the image of an uninterrupted life, the dignity and the advantages of an uninterrupted success; while his rebellious heart beat violently within his breast, as if maddened by the desire of a certitude immaterial and precious – the certitude of love and faith. What of the night within his dwelling if outside he could find the sunshine in which men sow, in which men reap! Nobody would know. The days, the years would pass, and... He remembered that he had loved her. The years would pass... And then he thought of her as we think of the dead – in a tender immensity of regret, in a passionate longing for the return of idealised perfections. He had loved her – he had loved her – and he never knew the truth… The years would pass in the anguish of doubt… He remembered her smile, her eyes, her voice, her silence, as though he had lost her forever. The years would pass and he would always mistrust her smile, suspect her eyes; he would always misbelieve her voice, he would never have faith in her silence. She had no gift – she had no gift! What was she? Who was she?… The years would pass; the memory of this hour would grow faint – and she would share the material serenity of an unblemished life. She had no love and no faith for anyone. To give her your thought, your belief, was like whispering your confession over the edge of the world. Nothing came back – not even an echo.

In the pain of that thought was born his conscience; not that fear of remorse which grows slowly, and slowly decays amongst the complicated facts of life, but a divine wisdom springing full-grown, armed and severe out of a tried heart, to combat the secret baseness of motives. It came to him in a flash that morality is not a method of happiness. The revelation was terrible. He saw at once that nothing of what he knew mattered in the least. The acts of men and women, success, humiliation, dignity, failure – nothing mattered. It was not a question of more or less pain, of this joy, of that sorrow. It was a question of truth or falsehood – it was a question of life or death.

He stood in the revealing night – in the darkness that tries the hearts, in the night useless for the work of men, but in which their gaze, undazzled by the sunshine of covetous days, wanders sometimes as far as the stars. The perfect stillness around him had something solemn in it, but he felt it was the lying solemnity of a temple devoted to the rites of a debasing persuasion. The silence within the discreet walls was eloquent of safety but it appeared to him exciting and sinister, like the discretion of a profitable infamy; it was the prudent peace of a den of coiners – of a house of ill fame! The years would pass – and nobody would know. Never! Not till death – not after…

'Never!' he said aloud to the revealing night.

And he hesitated. The secret of hearts, too terrible for the timid eyes of men, shall return, veiled forever, to the Inscrutable Creator of good and evil, to the Master of doubts and impulses. His conscience was born – he heard its voice, and he hesitated, ignoring the strength within, the fateful power, the secret of his heart! It was an awful sacrifice to cast all one's life into the flame of a new belief. He wanted help against himself, against the cruel decree of salvation. The need of tacit complicity, where it had never failed him, the habit of years affirmed itself. Perhaps she would help… He flung the door open and rushed in like a fugitive.

He was in the middle of the room before he could see anything but the dazzling brilliance of the light; and then, as if detached and floating in it on the level of his eyes, appeared the head of a woman. She had jumped up when he burst into the room.

For a moment they contemplated each other as if struck dumb with amazement. Her hair streaming on her shoulders glinted like burnished gold. He looked into the unfathomable candour of her eyes. Nothing within – nothing – nothing.

He stammered distractedly.

'I want… I want… to… to… know…'

On the candid light of the eyes flitted shadows; shadows of doubt, of suspicion, the ready suspicion of an unquenchable antagonism, the pitiless mistrust of an eternal instinct of defence; the hate, the profound, frightened hate of an incomprehensible – of an abominable emotion intruding its coarse materialism upon the spiritual and tragic contest of her feelings.

'Alvan… I won't bear this…' She began to pant suddenly, 'I've a right – a right to – to – myself…'

He lifted one arm, and appeared so menacing that she stopped in a fright and shrank back a little.

He stood with uplifted hand… The years would pass – and he would have to live with that unfathomable candour where flit shadows of suspicions and hate… The years would pass – and he would never know – never trust… The years would pass without faith and love…

'Can you stand it?' he shouted, as though she could have heard all his thoughts.

He looked menacing. She thought of violence, of danger – and, just for an instant, she doubted whether there were splendours enough on earth to pay the price of such a brutal experience. He cried again:

'Can you stand it?' and glared as if insane. Her eyes blazed, too. She could not hear the appalling clamour of his thoughts. She suspected in him a sudden regret, a fresh fit of jealousy, a dishonest desire of evasion. She shouted back angrily:

'Yes!'

He was shaken where he stood as if by a struggle to

break out of invisible bonds. She trembled from head to foot.

'Well, I can't!' He flung both his arms out, as if to push her away, and strode from the room. The door swung to with a click. She made three quick steps towards it and stood still, looking at the white and gold panels. No sound came from beyond, not a whisper, not a sigh; not even a footstep was heard outside on the thick carpet. It was as though no sooner gone he had suddenly expired – as though he had died there and his body had vanished on the instant together with his soul. She listened, with parted lips and irresolute eyes. Then below, far below her, as if in the entrails of the earth, a door slammed heavily; and the quiet house vibrated to it from roof to foundations, more than to a clap of thunder.

He never returned.

BIOGRAPHICAL NOTE

Joseph Conrad [Józef Teodor Konrad Korzeniowski] was born to Polish parents in Berdichiv in the Ukraine in 1857. His father, a landless gentleman, poet, and translator, was active in the Polish patriotic underground, which resulted in his imprisonment and in the family's exile. Once released from exile, his father soon died of tuberculosis and, from 1869, Conrad was supported by his uncle, Tadeusz Bobrowski, his mother having died two years previously. After school in Kraków, Conrad persuaded Bobrowski to let him join the French merchant marine with whom he was to travel to the West Indies several times between 1875 and 1878. His career continued in the British merchant marine, where he rose from common seaman to first mate, and, in 1886, he was given command of his own vessel, *Otago*. (It was also in 1886 that Conrad became a British subject.) His following years at sea were to prove vastly influential on his writing, as he sailed all over the world, and, most famously, up the Congo river in 1890, a journey depicted in his tale, *Heart of Darkness* (written 1899, published 1902).

Conrad settled in England in 1894, and married Jessie George in 1896, having published his first novel, *Almayer's Folly*, in 1895. Writing in his third language, Conrad did not achieve financial and popular success until *Chance* (1913), although earlier works such as *Nostromo* (1904), *The Secret Agent* (1907), and *Under Western Eyes* (1911) are held in greater critical esteem. Joseph Conrad died in 1924, and, after a brief period of neglect, was declared by F.R. Leavis as 'among the very greatest novelists in the language'.

SELECTED TITLES FROM HESPERUS PRESS

Author	Title	Foreword writer
Louisa May Alcott	*Behind a Mask*	Doris Lessing
Pietro Aretino	*The School of Whoredom*	Paul Bailey
Jane Austen	*Love and Friendship*	Fay Weldon
Aphra Behn	*The Lover's Watch*	
Anton Chekhov	*Three Years*	William Fiennes
William Congreve	*Incognita*	Peter Ackroyd
Joseph Conrad	*Heart of Darkness*	A.N. Wilson
Daniel Defoe	*The King of Pirates*	Peter Ackroyd
Charles Dickens	*A House to Let*	
Fyodor Dostoevsky	*Poor People*	Charlotte Hobson
E.M. Forster	*Arctic Summer*	Anita Desai
Nikolai Gogol	*The Squabble*	Patrick McCabe
Thomas Hardy	*Fellow-Townsmen*	Emma Tennant
Nathaniel Hawthorne	*Rappaccini's Daughter*	Simon Schama
Henry James	*In the Cage*	Libby Purves
Franz Kafka	*Metamorphosis*	Martin Jarvis
D.H. Lawrence	*Daughters of the Vicar*	Anita Desai
Leonardo da Vinci	*Prophecies*	Eraldo Affinati
Katherine Mansfield	*In a German Pension*	Linda Grant
Guy de Maupassant	*Butterball*	Germaine Greer
Lorenzino de' Medici	*Apology for a Murder*	Tim Parks
Robert Louis Stevenson	*Dr Jekyll and Mr Hyde*	Helen Dunmore
Jonathan Swift	*Directions to Servants*	Colm Tóibín
Mark Twain	*Tom Sawyer, Detective*	
Edith Wharton	*The Touchstone*	Salley Vickers
Oscar Wilde	*The Portrait of Mr W.H.*	Peter Ackroyd
Virginia Woolf	*Carlyle's House and Other Sketches*	Doris Lessing
Virginia Woolf	*Monday or Tuesday*	Scarlett Thomas
Emile Zola	*For a Night of Love*	A.N. Wilson